Y0-AQW-924

Faith, Hope and Homicide

By the same author

Death Beyond the Nile
A Kind of Healthy Grave
Grave Goods
No Man's Island
The Sting of Death
Funeral Sites
Captive Audience
The Sticking Place
Troublecross
Mrs. Know's Profession
A Charitable End

FAITH, HOPE AND HOMICIDE

Jessica Mann

St. Martin's Press
New York

 For information, address St. Martin's Press, 175 Fifth Avenue, New York, N.Y. 10010.

Library of Congress Cataloging-in-Publication Data

Mann, Jessica.
Faith, hope, and homicide / Jessica Mann.
p. cm.
ISBN 0-312-05427-0
I. Title.
PR6063.A374F35 1991
823'.914—dc20 90-49298
CIP

First published in Great Britain by Macmillan London Limited.

First U.S. Edition: February 1991
10 9 8 7 6 5 4 3 2 1

Faith, Hope and Homicide

Prologue

'There is blood on my hand,' Thea Crawford said.

She fumbled for a box of paper handkerchiefs, took several and began to scrub frantically at her palm. She said, 'Look, it's blood. But I didn't touch anything.'

'You must have.'

Thea was shivering, her lips trembled. She needed warmth, a drink and the comfort of home.

'Listen. I'm not hysterical. I'm never hysterical. You saw Louise too. She's dead. She's slashed her wrists. I didn't dream it. This blood isn't a dream. But I didn't put a finger on anything in that room. I am sure I didn't.'

Tamara Hoyland, who was Professor Crawford's friend and had once been her pupil, knew her to be clear-headed and unimaginative. She said, 'You could have done it without noticing.'

'No. I touched nothing in that room but there is blood on the palm of my hand.'

Welling up inside Tamara was a feeling of sickness, of despair such as she had never known. She folded her arms across her body, hands in her armpits. She did not give in to the instinct that would have pushed her down on to her knees, her forehead to the ground, foetally hunched away from the world, away from being seen, away from seeing, away from hearing the hideous thing that Thea was telling her. A wail inside her head, in her own mind, repeated again and again, 'Make it be a mistake. Don't let it be true. Let it be suicide, oh God, let her have killed herself.'

But murder was what it meant, that smear of blood, no longer on skin now, but a rusty mark on soft white paper. Someone else had been in that bedroom. Someone had killed her. Whether that person had cut the woman's wrists, or had found her bleeding to self-inflicted death, it was murder by omission or commission.

'If only we had got here sooner,' Thea Crawford said.

She and Tamara had driven round to the Waughs' house together in the evening, after Thea had finished writing the application for a research grant. While she worked, her concentration was absolute; now that her son was grown up, she had lost the knack of dividing her mind, half for her work, half for outside responsibilities, and Thea had made no attempt to entertain Tamara but simply told her to make herself at home. Thea's home, like its owner, was just beginning to show the signs of maturity. Thea had a diminishing interest in anything other than her subject, the most distant past, and it was some years since she had done any redecoration, but she was still a beautiful woman and her house still warm and welcoming.

Tamara Hoyland knew it well. An archaeologist herself, she would in other circumstances have spent a happy afternoon browsing in Thea's books, or, since she had wider interests than her friend, in the heaps of magazines and enticing new biographies and novels waiting for Sylvester Crawford's return from a journalistic assignment in America. But Tamara was uncharacteristically restless and could not settle to anything. She made coffee, did some yoga exercises, watched sport on television and wandered round the house until Thea complained of the interruption. Then she went out for a walk alone in the rain. Gloomily she had trudged up to the university and around its sodden, unspringlike grounds.

Once work was over, Thea decided to call in on Louise Waugh, usually known by her maiden name Louise Dench.

'I feel remorseful about her. I was too sharp with her the other day, and I should have remembered that she's been ill, quite apart from losing her husband. Come and keep me company.'

'All right. But I'll wait in the car. I don't want to see Louise again,' Tamara had said. Finer weather spreading punctually from the west brought some faint and watery sun to the streets of Buriton. The tourist season had not started yet, so the only place to find a suitable offering on a Sunday evening was a garage on the road to Penzance where Thea bought a pot of unseasonal Dutch chrysanthemums.

Tamara had been past the Waughs' house earlier in the day but not memorised the route, and Thea, who had lived in Buriton for years, moved in a restricted sphere and could only find her way with any confidence between the university, the town centre, the railway station and her own house. Eventually they had to return to the garage to ask for directions, and having found Gloweth Drive, View, Lane, Crescent and Avenue, had a lot of trouble in identifying Gloweth Terrace. Every house was white, with mono-pitch pink roofs. Under a Mediterranean sun the estate might have been charming. In the damp Cornish climate the metal-framed windows had quickly become spotted with corrosion, and the uniform design subverted by each house-owner's assertion of individuality, here a Georgian door, there a set of plaster mouldings or some classical, fibre-glass pillars around the storm porch. Some properties had smart little gardens, others untended patches. The Waughs' front strip had been covered over with tarmac. Beside each house was a garage. The streets were arranged around a common play area, its patchy grass spurned by the children who were wheeling around the road on bikes or roller skates.

Most of the houses had their windows masked by swags and drapes of variously patterned net. The Waughs' was exposed to view, and when there was no answer to Thea's ring she stepped to the side to peer into the one downstairs room. She saw modern furniture, used coffee mugs and a screwed-up handkerchief on the low table, over-full bookcases and piles of paper on the floor beside them; this was not a home where anyone troubled to plump the sofa cushions or set out artistic arrangements of ornaments. Thea walked back to her car and Tamara wound the passenger's window down.

'No answer?' she asked.

'You looking for Mrs Waugh?' A boy of about ten balanced on his skateboard at Thea's side. His shirt said that he belonged to the Houston Astros, but his accent was broad Cornish.

'Yes, do you know if she's gone out?'

'I think she's ill in bed. Her curtains are drawn.' He pointed to the upstairs window. It was open, its curtains billowing in and out in the wind.

'I wonder whether she's all right.'

'Dunno. Shall I get you the key?'

'Have you got it?'

'My mum has. She's gone out again. We went to see my nanna today.' The child skimmed across to the next house and around to its back door. He returned dangling a pair of keys.

'I'm not sure that Mrs Waugh would want me to . . .'

'My mum always lets herself in.' The chimes of 'Greensleeves' announced a suitable moment for Tamara to tip the child and he rolled rapidly down the hill towards the ice-cream van.

'What do you think?' Thea said.

'Go on in,' Tamara replied. 'I'll wait here.'

'I'll just leave the flowers with a note.' A little unwillingly Thea unlocked Louise Waugh's front door.

Inside the house, she called softly, 'Hullo? Anyone at home?'

Something was banging rhythmically in the wind. It was an obtrusive noise and must have been irritating to someone who was trying to rest. Thea wondered whether Louise had been taken really ill again. Still holding the keys in her right hand, the pot of flowers in her left, she went up the stairs. The narrow landing had a fitted carpet but no furniture. Doors led off it, one wide open to the bathroom, another ajar. 'Louise?' Thea said again. She could see through the gap that the irritating noise was caused by the wardrobe door banging to and fro in the draught. There was a curious smell, familiar yet unidentifiable.

Thea went cautiously into the room.

Almost without pausing and quite automatically she dashed out of it again, down the stairs and away from the house, gabbling incoherently about blood and death.

Tamara Hoyland had learnt to take disasters calmly. She pushed her friend into the passenger seat and went inside and up to the bedroom herself.

One glance was enough. Louise Waugh was dead.

She was lying on the bed, on top of a flowered, olive and ochre bedspread. A pair of yellow curtains flapped in and out of the window like sails. The wardrobe door moved backwards and forwards in the draught. Thea's pot of flowers lay broken where she had dropped it near the door, the earth spilled on to the beige carpet. There was a kitchen knife, lying on the floor below the blanched, dangling hand; and there was blood, poured out, soaking through, glistening in the evening light.

Tamara crossed the room, picking her way to one side of the wet patch on the floor. She touched the chilled flesh to confirm what was already obvious.

The telephone was in the downstairs room; she used it, was admonished to wait in the car and touch nothing in the house, and went out again to her friend.

Thea Crawford was slumped in the passenger seat staring at the palm of her hand.

'There was blood on my hand. And I didn't touch anything.'

She said it again and again. Her dark hair had escaped from its usual discipline, her naturally creamy skin was a sickly, skimmed-milk white.

'Blood. On my hand. From something in the house.' She would tell the police. She would say that she had touched nothing in the bedroom. She would be believed. There would be a murder enquiry.

Somebody had killed Louise Waugh. Hunched, crouched, hiding herself from the dreadful day, Tamara felt Thea's embrace. Thea said, 'I'm sorry. It's just as awful for you. I shouldn't have . . .'

Tamara had seen violent deaths before. It was not that which had caused her mind to go into frantic retreat, into mute refusal of the truth. Not the fact of death itself.

She forced herself upright, and said, 'Listen, Thea, it really matters. It's important. Please think again. Before they come, before the police get here, think about it carefully. Didn't you make sure she was really dead? Surely you must have touched her.'

In other circumstances Thea Crawford might have noticed the appeal in Tamara's voice. She said, 'I didn't. I dropped the flowers and ran. I suppose I held on to the banisters on the way down. There must have been a bloodstain on them. My hand wasn't on anything else in the house at all.'

Distant sirens were closing in.

The police would know what to think.

Tamara knew what to think.

She tried to wrench her mind away. She should be feeling sorrow for the dead woman. She should not be thinking about herself. Louise Waugh was dead. Concentrate on her.

Chapter 1

At the end of the previous May, four people had set off together for the jungle. Their research was paid for by the Grail Foundation. They all thought themselves lucky. Well qualified, and with complementary skills and shared interests, they posed for photographs, smiling against a lowering sky. The *Western Morning News* and Buriton's local weekly free-sheet printed the picture. Its title was 'Away to Adventure'.

Brazilian bureaucrats delayed them. It was the hottest time of year when the party was free to move on. Armand Rivière, the socio-linguist, had turned back before they even reached the wilderness. He had not realised how the climate and conditions would affect him, he said, pointing to the punctual column of mosquitoes that rose over the river banks at dusk, and the open sores on his leg, and the rash that mottled his chest. His previous experience of practical fieldwork had been in more agreeable surroundings to which he felt forced to return.

Louise Dench, the botanist wife of the geologist Robert Waugh, cut her leg badly while out for a stroll one evening. It was not an injury sustained in the course of selfless research, but an idiotic accident she could perfectly well have avoided. In the light shoes she had changed into after a day in boots, she had no protection against a rusting machete concealed by the vegetation. Louise took daily doses of blood-thinning drugs after having a thrombosis a few years previously. Her blood would not clot, the wound became infected, and she was forced to stay behind at a logging camp.

'I'll find a guide and follow you,' she told the others, but she became more feverish after they had gone, and was ill for a long time. She had no choice but to wait to be picked up by the other two on their way back.

But Alastair Hope returned from the jungle alone.

Robert Waugh had not survived the journey. Somewhere in uncharted territory he had died quite suddenly, from one moment to the next. Alastair was a doctor as well as a pharmacologist, but it was a long time since he had practised medicine. He hardly dared guess at a diagnosis. Had it been the bite of one of the deadly insects that infested the area? Had it been the result of eating some of the unfamiliar food their hosts provided? Was it a virus or a heart attack? The Indians had poison-tipped arrows, but Robert was unwounded. Could he have absorbed venom unawares, or perhaps touched one of the brilliantly coloured frogs, one hundred species of which secrete deadly toxins in their skin? The exudations of *Phyllobates terribilis*, as Louise knew, made strychnine look like table salt.

'It would have needed an autopsy to know what killed him,' Alastair explained. But that was out of the question; in any case Alastair did not possess the qualifications and the equipment to perform one. The tribespeople, he told Louise, believed that Robert had been the victim of witchcraft. They insisted on performing their own rituals to dispose of so dangerous a corpse.

'I couldn't even cut you a lock of his hair. They would not let me touch his body.' The only material relic of Robert Waugh that Alastair was able to bring for Louise was his backpack.

Alastair had not examined its contents, but scrupulously fastened the buckles on Robert's spare clothes, his notebooks, containers, even on the India paper editions of *Moby Dick* and *Barchester Towers*.

Alastair said that Robert might also have died if he had been within reach of a London teaching hospital. Louise was not convinced. If she had survived blood poisoning, he could too. All through their nine and a half years together, he had been far more robust than she.

Alastair said that the tribespeople had done their best.

Louise said that their best was not good enough. They were primitive people. What could one expect?

'They were kind,' Alastair said.

Kindness was not enough. Unskilled, uneducated kindness

had left Robert Waugh dead among those kind people.

Half dead herself, Louise was transported to England and taken directly from the airport to the Hospital for Tropical Diseases. Discharged, though not completely cured, she went home to Cornwall a month later.

She was relieved to have met nobody she knew either on the train or at the station. She dreaded explaining about Robert. She shrank from being told how poorly she looked, she winced at the thought of the practical help friends would offer. The neighbours would bring sympathy and flowers and ready-cooked casseroles. She cowered low in the taxi, keeping her face turned away from the window, and hoped that nobody would notice her homecoming.

The Gloweth estate was perched on a hill outside Buriton, where the ugliness of the little houses was redeemed by the magnificent view from their front windows, down across the wide sweep of the town and over the curve of the bay. Not many university people lived there; homes designed for young executives were above their means.

The Waughs' mortgage, now paid off by Robert's life insurance, had been serviced by their combined salaries. Neither of them would ever be able to move from Buriton to promotion in another university unless the other was also offered work in it. Widowhood had both enriched and released Louise, who, as a scientist, believed in facing facts.

The front door opened directly into the narrow, open-plan living room. The space was obstructed by the luggage that had been delivered while Louise was in hospital, her own green canvas, leatherbound cases, and Robert's nylon sausage bags and backpack.

Traces of the Waughs' hurried departure all those months before remained where they had been left. Louise could hear Robert's voice echoing in the empty room. 'Get a move on, we'll miss the train. Haven't you finished your packing yet?'

They had left the house while it was still dark outside, so the curtains remained half drawn as they had been that last morning. Two coffee cups, their dregs solidified and green, still stood on the hearthrug. The stained chair cover and the overflowing waste-paper basket were a reminder of the last row the Waughs had in this house, on the same subject as their first and most of those in-between: whose job was it to tidy up? Was he, was she, doing a fair share?

The diary was open at the last week in May. Leave for Brazil, flight VA256, mem. stop milk and papers, Robert had noted in his pernickety handwriting.

The house smelt of mould. The damp air struck Louise into uncontrollable shivers. She switched on the gas boiler, all the rings on the cooker, the electric blanket and both bars of the electric fire. She ached with exhaustion. Still wearing her coat, she flung herself on to the sofa, her head swimming. The waistband of her denim jeans was digging into her skin in spite of all the weight she had lost, and she unbuttoned and unzipped them, but still could not find a comfortable position. The cushion felt hard against her head, its inch-long tufts of hair chilly in comparison with the thick, pale ginger frizz she had worn ever since it was a political statement of feminism and freedom. The sofa, like everything chosen by Robert and Louise, was modern and utilitarian. It was very uncomfortable.

This won't do, she thought.

She forced herself up and went to the kitchen units at the back of the room. The refrigerator was empty; no milk. She poured some whisky into a cup of instant coffee. Was there anything to eat? Baked beans, powdered potato, pasta. If they had come back together Robert would have gone out for a Chinese or some fish and chips.

Louise was revolted by the idea of the only food at her disposal. The room was beginning to warm up, though still stuffy. She picked Robert's backpack from the heap of luggage and pushed the yellowed newspaper of two seasons before (headline: Holiday Washout) off the low table on to the floor. Unbuckling the straps she emptied the contents out. Some canisters of film rolled inaccessibly under the low-slung sofa.

The doorbell chimed. Louise took no notice. It was followed by a cooee through the letterbox and then the scraping of a key. 'Good dog, come on then, let's see who is here.'

Crouching with her back to the fire, Louise stared up at her neighbour. How buxom, how flushed, how healthy and alive she looked!

'Lou! I didn't know you were back. Welcome home. How was it? Oh—' She clapped her open palm over her mouth. 'Silly me, what an awful thing to say. Louise, I'm so sorry. It's so dreadful. But what happened? All we heard here was that Bob had passed away.'

Clearing her throat, Louise said, 'I didn't know you had a dog.'

'A— ? Oh that. I haven't, but I thought there might be intruders. The idea was to frighten them off.'

'It's very kind of you to—'

'Come on, tell me all about it. It's always better to talk. Don't hold things in, it doesn't help, I should know.'

Louise said, 'Is everything all right in Buriton?'

'Oh, Buriton's always the same, you know that. The Trewins moved out of number six, they are splitting up, but that's no surprise. And Molly Porter . . . but I'm forgetting, you won't know her. They only moved in last autumn. But do let me tell you what happened to the vicar. It was when he was organising the parade for Remembrance Sunday, and— oh, how awful, what am I thinking of? I shouldn't be rabbiting on like this, not when you look so miserable. But cheer up, where there's life there's hope, things will take an up-turn, see if they don't. You'll get over it.'

'Dora, to tell you the truth I'm half asleep,' Louise said. 'It's been a long journey. Would you mind terribly if I—'

'You don't look very well, actually. I didn't like to say anything about it. Are you all right? You don't think you have brought back one of those rare tropical diseases yourself?'

Louise said, 'No, I'm just tired. But you never know. Perhaps you'd better not come any closer just in case, and I'll see how I feel in the morning.'

'I ought to bring you something to eat,' Mrs Phillips said, retreating. 'I expect you're starving. Suppose I leave something in the porch?' She was torn between neighbourly goodwill, and fear of infection. But eventually she was persuaded to leave Louise be.

Chapter 2

As soon as she felt well enough to go out, Louise Waugh had Robert's reels of film developed. Then she had several sets of photographs printed. One set she showed to Ted Yule, the University's Lecturer in Anthropology. Another she gave to the Professor of Archaeology, and asked her to identify the subject.

Thea Crawford put them in the pile of papers she was saving to read on the train to London; there, without a mobile telephone and protected from having to listen to other people on theirs by a cassette player and headphones, she could be sure of nearly six uninterrupted hours. The combination of the Goldberg Variations, the dazzling marine views of south Devon and the incongruous details of the distant past proved gratifyingly fruitful, and she managed to draft a long, and long overdue article.

So the train was already on its final dash between Reading and Paddington when Thea took Louise's photographs out of her briefcase, and realised at a glance that she could not identify their subjects. She was interrupted by a colleague from Exeter University who had come to the front of the train to make a quick getaway. He was on his way to a protest meeting about university salaries, travelling on a cheap day return in second class, unlike Thea whose first-class fare was paid by the government department whose committee she was to attend that afternoon. She was embarrassed by her appearance of affluence, especially since it was not entirely inaccurate. She was infinitely better off than most academics, married to a television personality and with only one son, who was by now self-supporting. She felt obliged to let him distract her attention with chatter and to reaffirm her own support of the indignant scholars.

She took a taxi to the restaurant, where Tamara Hoyland had already arrived.

'Did you only come up this morning? You must have left Buriton at dawn,' Tamara said.

'So I deserve a good lunch,' Thea said. They ordered an exquisite, expensive and not-too-healthy meal, with pink champagne.

'How different from my usual lunch-with-a-girlfriend,' Tamara remarked.

'It's the only drink that leaves me fit to work in the afternoon,' Thea said.

'And you're wearing a Chanel suit.'

Thea accepted a plateful of scallops. 'I put this on because you're one of my few friends who will notice. We're feeling rich because Sylvester's doing a documentary series about civil wars, joint production with an American corporation. And I like your Jean Muir.'

They caught each other's eyes and burst into giggles. How many of their academic colleagues would have the faintest idea what they were talking about? Or, understanding it, react with anything but derision or contempt? But it was from Thea, then her tutor, that Tamara, as a post-graduate student, had learnt to take an interest in clothes, hairstyles, and the shape of a shoe. Thea, now the Professor of Archaeology at Buriton University, showed that elegance was not incompatible with the most severe scholarship. Indeed, the almost subconscious recognition of minute details that, added together, identified a dress designer, was not so different a technique from that used by an archaeologist to distinguish between types of potsherd. So Tamara was released from the puritan simplicities of her own contemporaries, who still, years on, gave the impression of seldom looking at themselves in a mirror, and of still regarding finery as unworthy and frivolous.

So, of course, it was, in comparison with the greater verities of real work, or with the lesser poverties of Thea's disaffected colleague on the train, or with the objective hardships voluntarily undergone by the man for whose delectation Tamara was at present choosing her clothes.

'So how's Alastair after all this time? And how did the Hope expedition go?' Thea asked. 'All I have heard is that Robert Waugh didn't survive it. Louise came back to Buriton at the end of last term looking like a ghost. Is Alastair all right?'

Tamara Hoyland and Alastair Hope had met for the first time at a dinner party given by the Crawfords. Tamara was spending the weekend with them in Buriton and Alastair had come down to discuss last-minute plans for their expedition with Robert and Louise Waugh.

Its main purpose was the search for specimens of medicinal plants that could be cultivated away from their natural rain-forest habitat. Trained as a doctor, with another qualification in pharmacology, Alastair was to travel with Armand Rivière, an expert in Amerindian languages, Louise Dench, a botanist, and her husband Robert Waugh, a geologist. The casual dinner-table chat could not hide the fact that Robert was included in the party only because his wife was indispensable to it.

Alastair Hope was dark and pale, with heavy lids to his eyes, long, thin features that would be gaunt in old age, and a wide, generous mouth. He looked like a man who was capable of emotion but always in control of it. His voice was deep, with traces of Scotland more in the intonation than the accent.

Meeting Alastair, hearing of his plans, Tamara found an image of herself in the jungle flashing into her mind.

'Do you need an archaeologist?' she said almost without thinking, and was immediately overcome by the knowledge of having said the wrong thing, a once-familiar species of embarrassment that should have been long forgotten by a successful professional woman of thirty. She felt her face redden, and turned away to Sylvester Crawford on her other side, whom she told at unnecessary length how little she really knew about South American archaeology. He listened with the observant attention of his profession, his eyes moving from her mobile, brightly coloured features to the swing of her light hair.

As Thea Crawford's student, Tamara had met the famous journalist and television commentator who was Thea's husband. He had made an automatic offer and she, well practised, had refused it without taking or causing offence. Tamara thought that Sylvester was amusing, agreeable and not entirely commendable; he thought it was a pity that such a pretty girl should take life so seriously. On that basis, they became good friends. They spoke easily together and neither of them needed to concentrate.

The spur to the evening's conversation had been Alastair Hope's 'shop', which ranged from the rigidities of modern science, through myth, legend, folklore and the varieties of cults from whose tiny seeds of sense he believed that new therapies could be developed.

'If there is one thing medicine needs to recognise, it's that there is often a basis of true memory for what otherwise seems to be the wildest nonsense,' he said.

'Not just medicine. What about the traces of a flood on Mount Ararat,' Sylvester said.

'Or Halley's Comet being the star in the west,' Tamara offered.

Thea interjected a scholarly denial that there was proper scientific evidence for either thesis. Undeterred, her guests continued to mention similar examples. But it was on Tamara that Alastair's attention was fixed and she, too, was almost uncomfortably aware of him. Once or twice she caught the amused, perceptive glance of Sylvester Crawford. It was not so long since he had unforgivably advised her to find herself a man and settle down.

'All very well to be a dashing single girl. Not so much fun to be a lonely old woman.' Was this evening's entertainment a masculine and patronising attempt at matchmaking? If so, it did not seem to have succeeded at first. Alastair and Tamara parted without making arrangements to meet again. But not long afterwards they were both, by coincidence, at the same Boat Race party in Chiswick. Afterwards they met by arrangement; at the opera, at a private view of some Venetian paintings and a publicity party for a television series.

Neither was inexperienced, both had learnt caution. Tamara had, in fact, lost her nerve after making the mistake, five years before, of falling in love at first sight with a man who turned out to be not just a thief and forger but a murderer too. It had been a mistake anyone could make. She knew that now, had known it then; but all the same, she had found herself unable to trust her own emotions afterwards. Until now; with Alastair she felt new-made, a young girl again rather than a worldly woman.

Not just her own personality but the times too had changed.

Ten years before it would have been bed first and dinner later. Now the ancient rituals of courtship were reviving. Before their first date Tamara prinked before her looking-glass like a Victorian debutante. Then, like an experienced twentieth-century career woman, she put clean sheets on her bed. And when Alastair came back from Brazil, it was into that bed and Tamara's home that he moved, instead of going back to the self-contained basement flat in Primrose Hill he rented from his sister.

It was not a secret, though Tamara had not realised that Thea Crawford already knew. But she would, of course; theirs was a small world.

Tamara said, 'Alastair is fine, thank you. But the expedition seems to have been disastrous. What with Robert Waugh dying and that Frenchman ratting before it properly began and Louise being too ill to do anything, Alastair's accounts of it are pretty depressing.'

'But he carried on alone, didn't he?'

'Of course, and he brought back a few specimens and a little information. It might turn out to be useful. But he found very little that wasn't already known. We are going down to Arthur's Castle at the weekend for him to confess to the sponsors. We might come over to Buriton, if Alastair needs to see Louise Waugh.'

'That woman has a bee in her bonnet,' Thea said, taking the packet of photographs from her bag. She fanned the glossy rectangles out on the table. 'These are the pictures Robert took before he died. She asked me to identify them for her.'

'Why you, Thea?'

'They are of an archaeological site.'

'Alastair never mentioned one,' Tamara said.

'This looks to me like Cuzco, or maybe somewhere in Peru. But I don't know a lot about it.'

Tamara spread the pictures out on the white damask. 'I have learnt a bit more about South American archaeology since I met Alastair. You're right, it is that sort of . . . but what about this statue? And this gateway – I must say, Thea, I don't recognise them.'

'Louise says that Robert took these photographs when he was in the jungle with Alastair Hope.'

Many of the pictures were shots of a ruined city. In some, great slabs of stone loomed above the camera. Beside an arch stood a child wearing few clothes, with stripes of paint on his cheeks and a gap-toothed smile, and an old man whose lower lip was grotesquely stretched around a large round disc. The scale of the structures was cyclopean. There were photographs of fallen pillars and blocks of masonry, others of houses made from vast cubes of stone, tightly fitted together, with carved porticoes, narrow above and wide below.

A wide-angled shot was of an open square, around which ruined buildings and standing structures were overgrown with riotous vegetation. It did not conceal everything. In the centre of the square was a tall column. A close-up showed that it was made of black, shiny stone. On top of it was a statue of a man, his arm outstretched, finger pointing.

'I don't recognise this,' Tamara said.

'What about these then?' Thea asked. She pushed other images to the top of the heap of pictures; small men, women and children, hardly clothed, carrying primitive weapons; a detail of the thick paint on a scarred cheek; a tiny child, grinning under a wide-brimmed hat with a striped band.

'That's Alastair's hat,' Tamara said.

'Are you sure?'

'It's the one he was wearing when I met him at Heathrow. Yes, I'm sure.'

'But he hasn't told you anything about visiting an archaeological site?'

'He wouldn't necessarily mention it, if it was somewhere on the tourist trail.' Tamara drank the last of the champagne. She said, 'It probably never occurred to him.'

'I have to go. I've got a meeting,' Thea said.

'What are you going to say to Louise Waugh?'

'I'll do a bit more research before I make up my mind. If it were anything exciting, Alastair would have known you would be interested. He would surely have told you, Tamara,' Thea Crawford said.

Chapter 3

Ben Oriel returned to Arthur's Castle after the winter with an increased appreciation of the place and a more educated understanding of what lay beneath it. He had always been aware of the power that suffused the soil, and been sensitive to atmosphere and emanations.

Since he had taken part in the New Age course near the Land's End, at the edge of Lyonesse, Ben had refined his perceptions and learnt to harness his innate powers.

Before putting on his uniform to go to work, he stood on the threshold of the cottage, communing with his mother, the Earth. No longer a novice, he did not need the support of the others with whom he had practised the technique. Standing in a circle around a sacred stone still energised by the initiates of antiquity who had left it as a beacon for future generations, they had raised their hands, palm to neighbour's palm. Eyes closed, they listened to the Earth. 'Can you hear it? Can you feel its warmth?' their leader prompted. 'I do, I do,' they replied in unison. Ben, a star pupil, could achieve the tingling heat in his fingers and hear the music of our sphere on his own, without needing the others' support.

He had returned to this place of power with a task imposed by the course leader, an adept endowed with the Third Eye. Justinian had shown that it was the role of the few people who both understood the urgency of the need and had the ability to meet it, to renew and to harness the Earth's energies. They would save the world.

Ben Oriel had been a student at Buriton University when he first understood that his life must be dedicated to the service of the planet. He did not stop learning; but he no longer needed to learn from hidebound academics.

His first achievement was the recognition of his own personal animal friends. He had opened his whole self to them during a ceremony of dreamweaving. Along with other neophytes he sang and chanted in unison with the Rainbow Warriors of the Sundance. The ritual took hours. At last it led him to union with his personal cognate creature. He felt his symbiote, a bat, dropping into his belly.

After that, it was no surprise to follow the greater horseshoes' flight last summer and discover their roost in the lean-to shed behind this cottage. It was *meant*.

The cottage was derelict when Ben came upon it and, although he now thought of it as home, outsiders would still regard it as a ruin. Ben's mother had been dismayed by the primitive circumstances he was living in.

She had found it hard to imagine that a whole family had once survived in such a tiny space. The house had been erected in the days when a Cornishman might lay legal claim to a plot of land if he could build walls and roof on it between sunrise and sunset. It had been deserted for years and even before that only used as a cow shed. The sole traces of human habitation were a three-legged metal cauldron with a triangular chip out of its rim, which Ben found lying on the mess of feathers and droppings in the hearth as though a witch had once stirred her potions there, and a blackened spoon, which he had taken from beneath a broken floorboard and stuck ceremoniously into the cracked door frame.

Ben's employer had ended the farmer's grazing lease. Since then brambles, ivy and in summer nettles and bracken grew over the dry-stone walls, and few slates were left on the broken beams. Nature was reconquering the man-made intrusion and after another few years only an expert eye would detect that it had ever been there at all. Even now, it was invisible from more than a few yards' distance, and the lean-to shed behind it would remain concealed until Ben had time to slash away the brambles and elder trees.

The man who built this hovel must have known what lay beneath it. It could not have been mere chance that led him to set his home on the very spot where the earth's energies surged like high tide, to sink his well where the sacred water had collected since distant antiquity.

Standing on the focal point of a ley line, Ben wondered again how other people could remain insensitive to the waves and gusts of power that swept over this rocky headland.

Ben's employer, at least, felt it. That was why he had established the Foundation here, dressing up his notions with a lot of romance about King Arthur and the Holy Grail. He was capable of enlightenment, and it was Ben's task to set him on the right road, to turn this place in the right direction. This was a place for re-forging the connection between the focuses of power that ranged from sites like Stonehenge and St Paul's Cathedral to Lake Titicaca in Peru. It was not by accident that Ben had first come to Arthur's Castle. He had work to do.

Ben looked down the brownish-green sweep of the valley to the sea, steely calm now, but with stripes of cloud that warned of wind before dawn. One of the modern world's pollutants was interfering with the atmospheric silence, a helicopter buzzing away to the west on its journey to RAF St Mawgan. Ben whispered a mantra to close his ears to it.

He put the binoculars to his eyes, but the Castle was guarded against observation with mirrored glass in the landward windows, and he could see nobody moving on the lawns or battlements.

At Christmas his mother had shown him a cutting from the *Guardian*, a paragraph of ill-informed gossip about the alterations to Arthur's Castle.

'It sounds fascinating, darling,' she said in her social manner. 'Can't you get me some details? I could use it in a novel.'

'Grown men come to play games,' Ben had told her. 'They dress up and enact scenarios. You wouldn't be interested.'

She probed further. The place was the property of a Trust established by Merlin Lloyd, an old, sick man. He, an Australian, came to Cornwall in the spring and went south in the autumn, and referred to himself and his fellow trustees as members of the Fellowship of the Round Table.

'What's in it for the others?' Ben's sister Pippa asked. 'Money?'

'Not necessarily,' their mother said. 'Some men take role-playing terribly seriously. Even your father used to go in for

Roundhead and Cavalier war games. It was a very expensive hobby.'

'The people at Arthur's Castle are insensitive clods. They invent their silly fantasies and don't see what is lying under their feet,' Ben said. As usual, any mention of his own creed and expertise caused his relations to change the subject, embarrassed by his sincerity as they were by anyone's true faith. They were not comfortable in the presence of clergymen either. They blushed and swivelled their eyes away when Ben mentioned those things that were not dreamt of in their philosophy.

It was becoming impossible to tune the noise of the helicopter out and when Ben looked up he saw that it was flying very low over the headland, buzzing the castle. He stood up, trying to see its markings through the binoculars. Surely they weren't allowed . . . it was coming towards him, slow and low. There was only one patch of land on the estate on which it could land, the flat, rabbit-nibbled turf that had once been the cottage's vegetable garden, just where Ben had been sitting. Crouching, he scuttled towards the shelter of the cottage itself, as the small yellow machine sank noisily towards the ground.

The whirlwind blew grit into Ben's eyes, and through blurred vision he saw a figure jump lithely down. There was a delay while the passenger moved into the pilot's seat and then the helicopter rose straight up into the air before moving away to the south-east.

'Don't rub your eyes, boy, it makes it worse.' The tone of experienced authority made Ben drop his hand from his face without thinking. 'Take my bags, will you?'

Blinking through tears, Ben bent to pick up two leather cases.

'Benjamin Oriel, right?'

'Benedict, actually. But everyone says Ben.'

'Right then, Ben, you can bring these along. Been waiting for me long?'

'Nobody told me you were coming.' His vision cleared, Ben saw that the new arrival was Count Kowalski, one of the Knights of the Round Table. At the previous season's banquet he had referred to himself as Sir Hector and sported chain-mail hired from Berman's, but now he wore the kind of smart-shabby suit that, along with the gleaming brogues and a tie in a code readable by those in the know, were a class indicator of the type that Ben had been brought up to recognise.

The Count led the way across the hillside to the path, his thornproof tweed impervious to overgrowth and undergrowth.

'Typical,' he said. 'Did they order my car?'

'I don't know, I'm afraid.'

The Count took a small telephone from his coat pocket. 'If you want something done properly, do it yourself,' he said, tapping out a long number. 'Take it from me, young man, it's a useful tip. Never rely on anyone else. You want something, go and get it. Want something done, do it. Wadebridge Garages? Kowalski speaking . . .' Without slacking in his stride, the Count barked out his requirements, sounded irritated to be told that they had already been met and stumped on towards the castle. Ben followed him with the two cases all the way to the front door, where Major Griggs came bustling out, glared at Ben's casual clothes and snatched the baggage away as though his hands were making dirty marks on it.

Back in the guard hut on the main road, Big Mac was taking things easy, playing with one of his electronic games, bleep-bleeping the cursor around the little screen with enthusiasm undiminished by habit.

'Sorry I'm late, I got caught by one of the guests.'

'Saw him. Come in the chopper, didn't he?'

'Are all the rest here now?'

'Yup,' said Big Mac. 'All except the pair from London. You'd better put the gear on.'

The boss was particular about the guards' appearance. A term of the contract with the security company was that its employees would be seen in full uniform at all times. Ben hung his own waterproof jacket with its non-regulation tartan lining behind the door and pinned the metal badge on to the epaulettes of the army sweater. Where the regiment's name should appear, a crest and tiny letters showed Safe Sure's insignia.

Ben had started to work for the company while he was a student, taking vacation jobs doing the security on building sites or in the national museums that employed private contractors for the purpose.

It was not meant to be a lifework. But when he was sent

down from Buriton University his father had cut off his allowance. Alexander Oriel was a rich man. He accompanied his parsimony with homilies and reproaches. Ben had not seen his father for three years. His mother, living on a novelist's erratic earnings, could not afford to give him much.

Now it was worth staying in a dead-end job because it kept him where he needed to be, at Arthur's Castle. Most of Safe Sure's employees wanted the bright lights. Big Mac would probably stick the season out, having already found himself a girl doing a chambermaid job in Wadebridge, but she was a temp, and so would he be. Barry had already announced that he'd be off at the end of the month. Safe Sure were lucky to have one employee who liked the place and was prepared to play Major Griggs's military games.

The job was phoney. Ben heard his mother's voice in his ears, 'But, darling, suppose you have to shoot someone?'

'We're just for show. It's all fiction, like what you write.'

Ben's sister, who was into the destruction of capitalist society, wondered whether Safe Sure's clients were worth protecting.

Almost certainly not, Ben had agreed, knowing that he would not be much protection if they had been.

'I'll be off then,' Big Mac said. 'Take care.' His motorbike was hidden in the trees along the road. Ben listened to its roar disappearing in the direction of Wadebridge. He sat down in front of the row of television screens. They were supposed to show the perimeter of the grounds, but the cameras were often out of alignment, and on one screen nothing appeared except the sky, and number three was, as usual, on the blink.

Ben pushed Mac's electronic games and Barry's heap of pornographic mags out of the way to reach his own box full of back numbers of *The Ley Hunter's Journal* which he had found in a junk shop in Bude the week before. It should keep him going for a while.

It was a boring job, being in security. On one assignment at an art gallery the guards used to see how many labels they could switch before anyone noticed, and on building sites there were usually enough spare men to get a poker school going. Doing duty once at a vandalised cemetery with another student, Ben had relieved the monotony by dressing up in sheets and moaning.

There was nothing to do in the guard hut at Arthur's Castle but read. Ben thought he might even have passed his exams if he had moonlighted here in term-time. In fact, he was a failed Bachelor of Arts (Buriton) and most of the time he managed not to care.

At other times, the memory of rejection seized him with fury. How little they knew, the people who set themselves up to judge others: the establishment, the materialists, the land-rapists, the destroyers of the planet, the hard-faced profiteers who preyed on the environment. Not as firmly in control as they liked to think, they would be sorry for snubbing Ben Oriel, one day.

He was not powerless. He was, rather, empowered, capable of doing things that would serve his cause and protect the planet.

'You couldn't hurt a fly,' Pippa had jeered during their arguments at Christmas. 'You look like a little boy,' she added more affectionately, dropping a kiss on his short brown curls and another on his ruddy cheek. Two years his junior, Pippa was married and had two children. Sometimes she treated Ben like another of them.

But Ben Oriel, at twenty-four, was no longer a child. He was a man. Others looked to him for action. Last season at Land's End it was Ben who had driven off some mocking tourists whose jeers were interrupting a ceremony of symbiosis with the Earth. It was Ben who had been able to finish off the dying rabbits whose blinded, red eyes and twitching limbs paralysed the other participants, it was Ben who had dealt with the farmer who had introduced myxomatosis.

Fools might suppose him to be the cannon fodder of the education system, going blindly into destruction, but they had got him wrong. He knew more than they supposed; and more than they knew themselves. Even here, at the Grail Foundation, where Ben was as invisible as the servants who once maintained the property, here too he knew more than anyone thought he knew; heard more than he was meant to hear.

Camera five showed a car turning off the main road towards Arthur's Castle. Ben checked his reflection in the chipped square of mirror and stepped out of the wooden hut to greet the new visitors.

Chapter 4

Alastair fiddled with the car's de-misting controls. Then he took a bright pink scarf from the pocket of his waterproof waxed coat and wiped the inside of the windscreen.

'Hey, that's mine,' Tamara said. She had left the scarf in Alastair's coat after borrowing it to scuttle through the downpour to the lavatories at the Exeter service station. He had put it on when he stopped on the Okehampton bypass for the same purpose. 'Here, use these.' She passed him some paper handkerchiefs, and he pushed the sodden silk back into his pocket.

Through the downpour an encampment of derelict vans and tepees could be seen on the cliff top. A tattered banner flapped by the gate. Tamara made out the word 'Peace'.

Alastair said, 'We should be nearly there. Can you look out for the turning any minute now?'

'I think it's round the next bend. Yes, this must be it.' The road was barred by a red and white striped pole, raised from within a gatehouse, through whose window a battery of electronics was just visible. A polite guard, in uniform as close to the military as the law allowed, checked their written invitation and identification.

It would not be difficult to devise a good security system for Arthur's Castle, thought Tamara Hoyland who knew a lot about such things, but this was not it. She began a mental list of the missing precautions.

'This place is supposed to be hard to penetrate,' Tamara said, not sure how much she would know about Arthur's Castle if she were really nothing but an archaeologist. It was, in any case, almost impossible for her to maintain with Alastair Hope the discretion of years.

His absence, which followed so soon upon their first meeting, had had the unexpected effect of bouncing them straight from the stage of mutual discovery to that of familiar intimacy. They had not slipped gently from one state to the next. When Tamara met Alastair at the airport, it felt like her homecoming as well as his.

'Used you to find you could swim much better at the beginning of summer than at the end of the one before?' Tamara said.

'In my case it was languages. I spoke them more easily at the beginning of each successive visit to a country, without any practise in-between. I think it's a subconscious consolidation of what one knows.'

He had followed the train of thought, as he unfailingly had done since their first meeting a year ago. They were as intimate as childhood friends, Tamara thought, and was immediately chilled by her own mendacious sentimentality. There was plenty Alastair had not told her; and plenty about her he did not know.

She had not liked to tell him what few people knew; that Tamara Hoyland, PhD, in fact and in public an archaeologist, had also been a secret servant of the State.

For several years Tamara had undertaken occasional assignments for an organisation disguised as an obscure section of the Department of the Environment, whose only entry in the reference books was under the uninformative name, Department E.

She had been recruited after the death of her lover, who worked for the department himself. Trained in arcane skills which she was usually careful to conceal, Tamara worked under the control, often little more than nominal, of Department E's director. Some jobs had been illicit, others dangerous.

Tamara's disguise was the truth, that she was an investigator working for the Royal Commission on Historical Monuments. Two years previously she had given up that job to write a book. But it had been depressing to recognise in herself an increasingly fierce cynicism. She doubted whether the destruction of her better self was a price worth paying for the achievements rewarded with the praise of powerful but anonymous men, and by large, unacknowledged payments into her bank account. Last year she had decided to give up her other job too, ceasing to be what danger and secrecy had made her. She intended to concentrate on dispassionate scholarship.

To Mr Black, who remained unconvinced, she said, 'I resign.' To her father, who alone of her family knew exactly what she had been doing, she said, 'I've retired.' To Thea Crawford, who had for years been pressing Tamara to complete a book-length version of her doctoral thesis, rephrased in terms comprehensible to a general reader, she said, 'I have really got going.' And to Alastair Hope she said, with more premeditation than at the first time of offering, 'If there's any chance you might need an archaeologist on your next expedition, I could learn up enough about the speciality to qualify.'

Now Tamara pushed aside the thought that brought Alastair's expedition and archaeology together. She had been trying not to think about it since lunch at Boulestin's with Thea Crawford. She wanted to enjoy herself without any of that old, familiar suspicion, without any of the searching for hidden meanings, the acceptance and analysis of intuition, that had been so large a part of her earlier career. She wanted to throw herself wholeheartedly, for a while at least, into being what their hosts at the Grail Foundation called Dr Hope's Significant Other.

It was in that role that Tamara had been invited to Arthur's Castle. The phrase provided for all contingencies. He could have been accompanied, they guessed, by a man, a monster or an animal.

It was rare for Tamara to be ancillary rather than principal. She looked forward to acting the part with gusto, and the more so because of the coincidence that Mr Black had once suggested that she should go to Arthur's Castle. He had rung to say that it would be just the job for her. 'Talk your way in. There must be some law that gives archaeologists a right to see ancient monuments. You would like to see the unrecorded antiquities, wouldn't you?' he offered, as though he were doing her a favour. 'You want to know what's there, I want to know what's happening there. Some of the people that go down . . . it's not just war games in fancy dress.'

'Yorkists and Lancastrians? Cavaliers and Roundheads?'

'Arthurian Knights of the Round Table actually. But I don't believe that's what they all go for. Not men like Hubert Blair and Jack Collin. There's something else going on.'

'Who does it belong to?'

'It's a Trust. The Grail Foundation. All perfectly legal and above board as far as the documents go. But some of the guests there . . .'

'Do you have any grounds for suspicion?'

'Only my sense of smell. I couldn't justify an operation. For all I know it's all completely innocent. But I'd like to be sure why Count Hector Kowalski and Professor Fleury Adams think it's worth dragging themselves to the back of beyond three times a year. The local constabulary are curious too.'

It was not good enough. Not even to see what remains of antiquity were still visible at Arthur's Castle would Tamara work for Department E again. She had finished with subterfuge.

Tamara had hardly spoken to Mr Black since. She had heard nothing from Department E. She had put it out of her mind, and the only trace of the change the experience had made in her was that she still kept herself in physical trim, carrying on with the exercise that had been prescribed by a tough anonymous trainer whose brief had been to keep her in top condition.

She wondered whom Mr Black had sent to Arthur's Castle in the end, and in what disguise. She was glad to have been free to come without one, though she had asked Alastair not to use her academic title. But there was some archaeological equipment in the boot of the car. Study of Arthur's Castle had been prevented by its present owners and there was plenty she meant to look at while she was there if she had the chance.

The invitation was scrutinised by men and machine and pronounced acceptable.

'Drive straight on, sir, without pausing. Major Griggs will meet you at the bottom.'

'Major Griggs?'

'The castellan,' the young man replied, deadpan.

A narrow road wound down through the valley past ancient stunted oak trees and overgrown ferns. Bridges made of stone slabs led across a clear, fast-running stream. The rain suddenly paused. A rainbow arched picturesquely ahead and dripping leaves glinted against a fugitive ray of evening sun. This pretty wilderness had been cultivated once. Camellias and magnolias had grown into a barrier not quite thick enough to hide a multi-stranded barbed fence.

The road came out from between the trees on to an area of tarmac. Beyond it was a shingle beach between two arms of cliff. To the right it was vertical and inaccessible. On the left, the west side, stairs twisted up towards a narrow neck of land beyond which was the promontory on which Arthur's Castle stood.

Surmounting the grey stone like a larger natural outcrop, the castle's smoothed granite blocks grew up from the rough bedrock without a visible break. At sea level those jagged teeth on which so many ships had foundered echoed the silhouette of the crenellations far above. A single tower jutted highest of all.

'Just leave your bus here, we'll put it away for you later.' The man was so obviously a retired Major that he must be doing it on purpose. He had pink, well-fleshed skin and very clear pale blue eyes. When he spoke his small grey moustache bobbed up and down like a glove puppet's jaw.

He gestured to a row of double doors, on the ground floor of a two-storey stone house, built right up against the cliff. It might once have been a fish cellar. The upper windows reflected the setting sun.

Alastair and Tamara got out of the car. They shook hands with the Major, who performed a semi-military semi-salute. 'Is that where we're staying?' Alastair said.

'No, Dr Hope, you'll be in the castle. Up and over. You can walk if you like, or go up in the lift.'

'Lift?'

'In the rock. There's a tramway. They say the shaft was tunnelled by unemployed miners. A sort of nineteenth-century job creation scheme.'

'We'd rather walk.'

'Good, have a bit of fresh air. Driven all the way from London, have you? Need to blow the cobwebs away. I'll keep you company if I may.'

The steps and their handrail were cut from the solid rock face. It was a steep climb. They emerged panting on to a narrow stretch of land which led across towards the wider area, not quite an island, on which the castle had been built.

Tamara said, 'What's a castellan?'

'The governor of the castle. I am in charge here, for my sins.'

'What does that involve?'

'I'm just a glorified dogsbody. Jack of All Trades, that's me.'

The front door was up a flight of semicircular steps. Looking back from it, Tamara saw high cliffs running along the coast, a startling and unfamiliar seagull's-eye view of black rocks, white-stained with guano and fringed at the top with green.

'Welcome, welcome to Arthur's Castle,' Major Griggs said solemnly. They followed him indoors.

No photographer had been permitted to publish, perhaps even to take, pictures of the interior of Arthur's Castle since it became the Grail Foundation's property. But it was known that Guyler and Ghosh had won the contract to do the interior design, and Tamara, who had seen illustrated articles about other commissions they had undertaken, immediately thought, 'Of course. I should have guessed.'

The building was not ancient, though its site was famous as a legendary fortress of the Once and Future King, Arthur himself. It was undeniably an Iron Age fort. The castle was erected in the early nineteenth century by a romantic architect whose notions of *La Vie de Chateau* derived from Sir Walter Scott. He had supplied galleries for minstrels and tilting grounds for extinct feats of chivalry. There were balconies for maidens to lean from and for swains to scale, as well as glory holes for heathen prisoners, slits for shooting arrows out of and spits for roasting oxen.

Intermittent alterations by owners more interested in the grandeur than the comfort of their status symbol had made little impression on the powerful master plan of a folly built to withstand a siege. *Country Life* had published photographs just after the war showing a bleak, underfurnished pile which had never recovered from being requisitioned in 1940 to house prominent prisoners of war. After that it was not used at all except for a short while as a coastguard's look-out.

What the Grail Foundation bought was not much better than a ruin. But its position was spectacular and popular. Immediate objections were registered from walkers no longer permitted to use the Foundation's stretch of the coastal footpath, from archaeologists prevented from examining the prehistoric remains, and from the North Cornwall District Council, whose policy was to discourage the residential use of remote country properties on the grounds that they were inconvenient for the emergency services, school buses, dustbin collections and home helps.

In reply the Foundation promised that nobody with children at local schools would ever be employed and any employee who became pregnant would be sacked. An outcry from a local feminist organisation and from the Trades Unions ensued. The trustees promised never to make use of local authority services and always to incinerate their own garbage. The conservation groups said that would pollute the atmosphere. The local Planning Committee refused permission for change of use, and the Secretary of State overruled them and granted it.

So far, so well documented. But recent gossip had produced little hard fact about the place. Most references or descriptions consisted of guesswork. The *Daily Express* printed what were said to be leaked copies of the Guyler and Ghosh drawings, which showed Arab-style courtyards and divans with a lot of mosaic decoration. *The Times* wrote that Ghosh had been overheard at the Garrick Club talking about matching a castle on a coast with the chastity of classical columns and pure white draperies. Paestum was said to have sprung to his mind. Meanwhile Guyler was known to have gone on a research trip to Peking.

Neither chinoiserie nor classical influence nor traces of the mysterious East were to be seen.

Guyler and Ghosh had asked themselves what mediaeval kings would have wanted in their palaces if knowledge and technology had been able to provide. They concluded that warmth and colour would have been the chief desiderata, occasionally and imperfectly available to the rich and dreamt of by the poor as promises for the next world.

The castle door opened on to heat and technicolour. Without visible radiators, and with only one tree trunk sulkily smouldering in the open hearth, the temperature was anachronistically that of a hothouse. High, narrow windows were obscured by rich-coloured, heavily leaded glass but brilliance from concealed sources flooded the hall. The floor, at first sight covered with loose laid rushes, was in fact a very long-piled velvet carpet. Vividly coloured tapestries hung over the walls, the embroidery garishly unfaded. Seats were draped with lengths of crimson and purple cloth, printed with gold design and tactfully masking a cushioned comfort.

The general impression was remarkable, and Tamara and Alastair obediently gasped.

'Quite something, what?' said Major Griggs.

'Breathtaking,' Tamara agreed.

'Have to remind you about the agreement you signed. No photographs, no filming, no subsequent publications. Breach of confidence, breach of contract, right? Good, well, that's out of the way. Come you in, we'll go straight up. The dressing bell went fifteen minutes ago. Dinner at twenty hundred. And we dress. Black tie.'

The stairs were made of hard, brilliant stones like malachite and cornelian, laid in slabs beside smooth and mysteriously warm marble. The passage walls on the second floor were decorated with a mosaic design of peacock feathers. Each door, made of slabs, or at least veneers, of alabaster, was labelled. Tamara and Alastair were given rooms on the same corridor, but separated by several others.

'Here we are, this is for you, dear lady. Guinevere's Chamber. Dr Hope is in Sir Bedivere. Let me see, has someone brought . . . Yes, all present and correct. I don't want to hurry you, dear lady, but we try to keep things to schedule. Do join us in the solar as soon as you are ready.'

The tapestries in Tamara's room depicted a maiden and a unicorn, in much brighter colours than the familiar original. The bed was draped with green silk. A semicircular window facing west gave on to an immense view of coast and ocean. In this riot of Hollywood-style archaism, Tamara was almost relieved to see the orange glare of a Cornish tourist resort against the dusk.

What had the designers done about that unmediaeval convenience, a bathroom? A door painted in trompe l'oeil as a figured velvet curtain opened into a closet, elaborately fitted with looking glasses and spotlights in the form of candelabra. The turret on the other side of the room, perhaps designed for a privy that dropped its ordure directly to the sea below, contained a plumbed-in throne and a circular gold bath deep enough for a lady to sit upright within her modest tent of cambric. Above it hung a silver pitcher held in a carved stone hand that protruded from the wall. Tamara experimented with the spout and handle. Hot and cold water gushed as though poured by a maidservant.

On the dressing table, inconveniently in the shape of an oak coffer, was a leatherbound, gilt-clasped book which turned out to be not a bible but an information pack. Tamara followed instructions to find a telephone concealed in a little shrine, a small, well-supplied refrigerator behind the carved front of a court cupboard and a television set in a dome-topped leather trunk.

The atmosphere was not so much that of a luxurious hotel as of a millionaire's yacht, chartered by rich strangers and used as they would use hotel rooms, but still retaining something of the personality of the owner and exerting some of his influence. Tamara longed to meet the man for whom this exotic and anachronistic palace had been created.

Alastair was nervous about meeting him – not that he had said so, but Tamara sensed that he was dreading the moment when he told his sponsors that he had returned empty-handed from the expedition they had paid for.

In exchange for the money, the Grail Foundation had the rights and the copyrights in all the information he brought back. But there was hardly any. 'Do you mean you aren't free to publish your results?' Tamara had asked.

'It isn't as though I found anything new anyway,' he had said.

'But what about scientific censorship then?' Tamara and Alastair, so quickly intimate, still had gulfs of ignorance about each other.

'I tend to be pragmatic about that kind of thing. I have nothing to tell them, so it doesn't matter if I can't tell the world.'

Tamara had been born a non-conformist. The tendency had been nurtured by her education, during the years when students were by definition rebellious, and later by her experiences in the questioning, self-reliant world of secret activities. An instinct told her that Alastair was wrong, although she knew that research funded but unpublished was probably better than a brilliant scheme for publishable research that was never carried out because nobody would pay for it.

'If I'd found anything of benefit to mankind, the Grail Foundation would be the first to develop it,' Alastair said. 'They mean well. Honestly.'

Tamara had no reason to doubt it. All the same, there was something about the set-up here that irked her.

Her hand on the door, she paused, momentarily analysing her own feelings. Was she suspicious, frightened, shy, bored? As when getting flu one feels mild aches and pains without at first noticing them, Tamara was aware of something wrong with her reaction to Arthur's Castle. If I were a dog, she thought, my hackles would have risen. More than the decor was phoney here.

She walked along the corridor to Alastair's room. He was sitting on the edge of his bed (interior sprung, but disguised as a portable campaign pallet), hooking together his bow tie.

'How I bless black velvet,' he said. 'Did you know that it's all right to have a made-up tie if it's made of velvet? When I think of the miserable sessions failing to tie a bow I used to endure before I discovered them.'

'A shaming social deficiency,' Tamara said. 'Should you be telling me such things? How can I ever respect you again?'

'Well, I certainly wouldn't tell Major Griggs.'

'What's the betting he is in full dress uniform?'

Laughing, they went down to dinner together.

Chapter 5

Thea delivered the report to Louise Waugh herself, calling in at her office after a Senate meeting that had been even more frustrating and boring than usual. Responsibility without power was the ruin of university life, a colleague had muttered during an inconclusive argument about fees for foreign students, and Thea's doodle was the rough draft of a letter of resignation. When she left, she was careful to pocket the scrap of paper. Even she did not know if she meant it.

The vacation had begun, but a good many students were still hanging around. Louise would not be officially at work until next term but several of her pupils had come in to ask about their own work or to offer their condolences. Her office was full of cards of sympathy, and beribboned pots of hyacinths scented the hot, dry air.

The newer science departments of Buriton University were in a 'temporary' cabin erected ten years before and now well settled into the ground. It was hot in summer and cold in winter; in early spring the western gales whistled through gaps in the planking, causing the thin softboard lining to buckle and crack. But the windows faced the sea; and coming into the room Thea was momentarily dazzled by the familiar but always remarkable view down across the roofs of Buriton and round the curve of sand to the domed observatory and the bright white lighthouse beyond. A fleet of fishing vessels from Eastern Europe had taken shelter from the previous night's storm, and privileged crewmen brought an exotic aspect to the little town as they jostled through Fore Street and Market Square to buy carpets and clothes. With so many ships in harbour the scene looked as it must have done when Buriton Bay was the centre of a local shipping and fishing industry before sailing dinghies became the only regular traffic on the bay.

Louise was sitting with her back to the window. She looked more collected than she had early in the week and was already putting on some of the weight she had lost during her illness. Big boned and broad, she was not suited to the contemporary fashion for being very thin.

The *Guardian* Education Supplement lay on her desk, folded back at a page of University vacancies. Even upside down Thea recognised it. Any future post of her own would come by invitation rather than application, but like most academics she made a regular weekly check of the jobs advertised.

'I suppose you want to get away,' she said.

'Buriton's a backwater, isn't it? I want to go somewhere modern, forward thinking. I always did hate this atmosphere of being shackled by moribund tradition and bogus sentiment.' Louise was a native and graduate of Manchester; Thea recalled many jibes and jokes about effete southerners both from her and from Robert, who was originally from southern Scotland. 'I'm free to move now,' she said.

What she meant was too obvious to need explanation. The likelihood of Louise and Robert Waugh finding new posts at the same university had been infinitesimal. In fact, as far as Thea knew from university gossip, Robert would probably have been stuck at Buriton indefinitely. He had not published enough to compete with others who had lists of articles and books to their name. Without him, Louise would not have much trouble finding another, better job.

I wonder how long Louise would have gone on letting Robert hold her back, Thea thought. She would not have laid much money on the likelihood of the Waughs still being together in five years, if Robert had lived.

'As a matter of fact we were going to separate in any case,' Louise said. 'After the South American trip. It wouldn't have been fair to Robert if I had let anyone know before that.'

'You don't have to tell me.'

'I wouldn't, except that you don't give a damn. If a clergyman or social worker came near me I'd run a mile. In fact I nearly did, when the vicar came to call last week. You are so elegantly disinterested, Thea, uninterested too, I should think. Other people's secrets probably pour off you like water off a duck's back.'

Thea was hurt as she had once been when an enemy (in fact, one of Sylvester's ex-girlfriends) had called her a chilly prig. It was true that she did not have a naturally warm personality, as the self-awareness of adult life had taught her, and she cared less for people and more for her work as time went on. She lived by the intellect rather than by emotion. But she was capable of true love and real sympathy, if only towards her family and a few close friends, and she did not like the idea that other people could recognise the character defect. She raised her fine, dark brows and said coldly, 'What makes you think that?'

'I suppose because it's how I am myself,' Louise said.

There was a chipped oblong of mirror on the wall, between a notice-board covered with lecture timetables and the blown-up photograph of a microscopic specimen. Thea stood up to look at her own reflection with its disciplined dark hair, its perfectly painted complexion, its blue gaze, always and still (in spite of the gathering wrinkles, more apparent, Sylvester insisted, to Thea than to anyone else) deceptively dreamy and melting. What had she in common with her brash, unsubtle colleague? Turning, Thea looked speculatively at Louise. Was she, perhaps, suffused with the sex appeal that is invisible to other women? Something had given her that aggressive self-confidence. She doesn't like me, and I don't like her, Thea realised, though it was rare for her to make such analyses.

Louise went on, 'Clever women are probably all the same. Too much head, too little heart, Robert used to say. But then his problem was the other way round.'

'If your memories of your husband are so unaffectionate,' Thea said, 'why are you making such an effort about his relics? You seemed extremely anxious about these photographs.' She put her long fingers on the transparent folder she had brought with her. 'I thought all this was a kind of labour of love for you.'

'Not love, guilt.' Louise said. She got up and began to walk around the room. She still limped slightly, but her complexion was clearer and she had washed her hair; if only she took more trouble she might look quite presentable, Thea thought.

'Robert might have done better in industry or school teaching. He should never have tried to be an academic,' Louise said. 'He simply wasn't good enough, with the competition one faces these days. He didn't have what it takes, that spark, or flair. He was intelligent but not really sensible.'

'Some people would say that's exactly the qualification required for our ivory tower,' Thea said.

'Except that we don't live in an ivory tower any more, not in the sciences at any rate. Perhaps in your subject you still do.' There was a faint contempt in Louise's voice. Next she would be using the word 'relevant', Thea thought.

Louise said, 'We have to make our work relevant to the modern world. It's no use looking backwards all the time. Sponsors want a material return for what they contribute. Society needs evidence that there is some point in what we are doing. I kept telling Robert that.'

'Environmental studies are quite a practical discipline, I'd have thought.'

'If practically applied, certainly. I don't know whether Robert would ever have done much except talk. I suppose he was all right as a teacher. Anyway, there's no point in discussing that, it's all hypothetical. But I was married to him, after all, even if it was a mistake. Now he's dead I feel I owe it to him to make sure he gets the credit for what he did discover in the end. It would have made his name and he ought to be remembered for something.'

'For this lot?' Thea said sceptically.

'What do you think it is then?'

'I can't really say. But I'm no expert on South America, as I told you.'

Louise moved the newspaper aside to find a book stamped with the University library's crest. 'This is what someone saw in 1743. It was an expedition led by a Portuguese called Francisco Raposo. They were looking for the lost silver mines of Muribeca. You look at the photos while I read it.'

'Carry on.' Thea settled herself as comfortably as possible on one of the chairs of little-ease the university had mistakenly bulk-bought in the nineteen-sixties.

'This is about Raposo and his party reaching a high point

from which they saw a huge city about four miles ahead. The Indian scouts said it was deserted. "They followed the trail to an entrance under three arches formed of huge stone slabs. So impressive was this cyclopean structure that no man dared speak but slipped by the blackened stones as stealthily as a cat. High above the central arch characters of some sort were graven deeply into the weatherworn stone. Raposo, uneducated though he was, could see that this was no modern writing. A feeling of vast age brooded over everything and it took a distinct effort for him to issue in a hoarse unnatural voice the order to advance." '

'What are you reading from, Louise?'

'This is a book about Colonel Fawcett, the one who was lost in the jungle trying to find El Dorado. He learnt about it by reading this report of what Raposo said he'd seen.'

'Fascinating.'

'I'll carry on then, shall I? "The arches were still in a fair state of preservation, but one or two of the colossal uprights had shifted on their bases. The men passed through and entered what had once been a wide street, but littered now with broken pillars and blocks of masonry rank with parasitic vegetation of the tropics. On either side were two-storeyed houses built of great blocks fitted together with mortarless joins of almost incredible accuracy, the porticos, narrow above and wide below, decorated with elaborate carvings of what they took to be demons." '

Louise spread the photographs out on her desk. 'Look here,' she said. 'And here. It matches, doesn't it?'

'So far.'

'There's more. "There was ruin everywhere, but many buildings were roofed with great stone slabs still in position. Huddled together like a flock of frightened sheep, the men proceeded down the street and came to a vast square. Here in the centre was a huge column of black stone and upon it the effigy, in perfect preservation, of a man with one hand on his hip and another pointing towards the north. The majesty of this statue stuck deep into the hearts of the Portuguese and they crossed themselves reverently." '

Thea Crawford looked closely at the photograph Louise handed her. She had never been to South America, nor taken any but the most general interest in its past; but the excitement of discovery, an emotion seldom felt by an archaeologist for whom the subject was an intellectual challenge rather than a romantic quest, momentarily gripped her.

' "Carved obelisks of the same black stone, partially ruined, stood at each corner of the square, while running the length of one side was a building so magnificent in design and decoration that it must have been a palace. The walls and roof had collapsed in many places but its great square columns were still intact. A broad flight of ruined stone steps led up to and into a wide hall, where traces of colour still clung to the frescoes and carvings." And so it goes on,' Louise said. 'Descriptions of a place written in the middle of the eighteenth century, and never since found. But this is it. I'm almost certain of it. El Dorado.'

'Correct me if I'm wrong,' Thea said, 'but I don't believe that Colonel Fawcett was regarded as an authority. He wanted to believe in the lost city full of treasure, didn't he?'

'Contemporary authorities accept that there are many lost cities still to be found in Amazonia.'

'And no expedition has found one.'

'You don't seem to realise how huge the area is,' Louise said. 'It will be generations before it is all mapped or explored. There are still new species of flora and fauna being discovered every year. If I hadn't been ill I might have found one myself. And there are still isolated groups of Indians that have never had any contact with the outside world. There are people whose lives are unchanged from those their prehistoric ancestors lived, Thea, living archaeological specimens for you. Why shouldn't there be lost, abandoned cities too?'

'No reason. New discoveries about the past do turn up all the time even in areas of the world about which one would have thought there could be nothing more to learn.'

'That's exactly what I mean.'

Thea said, 'Let me get this straight, Louise. Do you believe that Robert came across Raposo's or Colonel Fawcett's El Dorado?'

'I believe that he and Alastair Hope found it, and that for some reason of his own Alastair hasn't admitted it. He wants all the Hope expedition's glory for himself.'

'If Robert found a site, whether it is the legendary El Dorado or any other, it's very important and very exciting. But where is it? After all . . .' Thea's voice faded as she took in what the problem was.

'After all, you were going to say, I wasn't there because I was in hospital. Robert was there and mysteriously died.'

'Mysteriously? What do you— ?'

'I'm not making accusations. I don't see how there could ever be any evidence. All I will say is that it was very convenient for the sole survivor. Alastair Hope is the only person who knows exactly where they went.'

'He's telling the sponsors about it this weekend. His girlfriend told me they were going to Arthur's Castle,' Thea said.

'What, without telling me? Let alone inviting me! He thinks I'll keep away and keep quiet, I suppose.'

'Could you add anything, considering that you were not able to go with them on the actual expedition?'

'I could certainly add a bit of truthfulness. What do you think Alastair Hope will be telling the Grail Foundation, Thea? One thing is for sure – it will not be where to find El Dorado.'

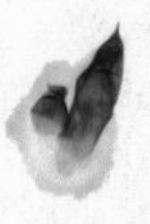

Chapter 6

Nobody sat at the head of the table, though a tall canopy without a chair beneath it marked the place of honour.

Tamara found herself sidling and simpering as her chair was held and pushed in for her. But I wouldn't be a damsel, I'd be a dowager, she thought; mediaeval maidens married at fifteen. For a moment she toyed with the vision of her prosperous elderly male companions in suits of armour instead of dinner jackets. It was the personnel who spoilt Guyler and Ghosh's period perfection.

'I rather think these should be solid bread trenchers,' Tamara said, looking at the silver-gilt plate before her.

'The cutlery is a bit of an anachronism too,' one of her neighbours replied. He had been introduced as Sir Hubert Blair, and looked so unremarkable, so colourless, so difficult to describe or even remember, that he seemed to have assumed a professional anonymity. But his notoriety had once been in direct disproportion to his influence; he was the epitome of an insider. This old man had never retired to his garden and the crossword puzzle.

Tamara peered down the solid oak board at which twenty people could comfortably have sat. 'The table is in period,' she said.

'And so is the serving wench,' said the man on Sir Hubert Blair's far side, putting out his hand to cup the girl's buttock without the slightest concealment. Tamara wondered whether the wages and job description included a suitably feudal complaisance, and glanced up at the girl, who responded with a very slight grimace. She wore a Hollywood version of peasant gear but the food made no concessions to historical authenticity, though the wine, or, for Count Kowalski, the whisky, was poured from gold flagons into gold beakers.

The Count's, unlike Sir Hubert Blair's, was a famous face. Those Slavic cheekbones and pale eyes were slightly smaller in real life than on the screen, more lined and blotched than they appeared under make-up; Tamara had not realised that Hector Kowalski was so old, though, having fought in the Second World War, he could not be much under seventy. He still looked at women with frank sexual interest, and still had an aura of power.

His fame had survived the dramatic end of his political career after a newspaper published photographs of him in bed with a trio of prostitutes. That must have been in the late nineteen-fifties. Somehow a glamour had attached itself to him, partly due to a notorious episode that had left a thin scar on his face, when he fought a duel against a rival in love. They had travelled to Morocco, where it was not illegal at the time, and used antique Saracen swords.

Abbreviated references in popular journals to 'the Count' were always understood as meaning Kowalski. Here was a dashing foreign nobleman, who had escaped dramatically to London in 1940, been decorated for his daring in secret operations in the Far East, married a film star, and been elected to Parliament. He would go far, commentators said; and the same prophets smote him with their ire when he broke the eleventh commandment and was found out. Even after he had resigned his seat, been divorced by the film star and become a businessman instead of a politician, he had still been written about, considered and admired.

The Count behaved like a very important person still though he had been ousted from the huge company he had once built up. Now he held a handful of non-executive directorships and lent his name to commercial or charitable organisations. He had been awarded a few honorary degrees and unveiled many commemorative plaques. He cruised the world in luxury, for which he paid by shaking the paying passengers' hands, signing autographs and delivering one or two lectures in the course of the voyage. He gave political opinions and charged for them. Recently he had led a list of International Champion Freeloaders published by a satirical magazine.

The Count spoke very little but Sir Hubert Blair was a man who knew his social duty.

He talked about skiing, opera, the road system between London and Cornwall (spinning the rival merits of motorways and dual carriageway by-passes out through half a course) and the artistic revival of naturalistic landscape painting. He did not ask Tamara what she did or mention the purpose of Alastair's visit.

A menu in front of each place, held in a small mailed fist and written in gothic script, informed the diners that the pudding was called Flummery Camelot. Count Kowalski stirred the bowlful dubiously, and Hubert Blair said,

'It's possible to carry period detail a little too far.'

Lord Collin, on Tamara's right, ate with absent-minded greed. He had sat through the meal chewing industriously and saying almost nothing.

Lord Collin of Riverside, formerly Sir John, and before that plain Jack Collin, was not quite a grand old man. A former cabinet minister, he had told an anonymous profile writer that he was one of the people who pulled the strings. But for some time he had been reduced to issuing his advice and recommendations through signed newspaper articles. It was seldom followed, or even discussed.

Tamara said, 'Do tell me about the Arthurian connection, Lord Collin. I suppose it all came about because of the castle's name?'

'It means a good deal more to us than that, lass.'

'I would love to hear about it.'

'You'd have to talk to Merlin to get the full picture.'

'That's Mr Lloyd?'

'You'll meet him tomorrow, I daresay.'

'But meanwhile . . . I suppose you are involved in it all.'

'I am a Knight of the Round Table.' His already florid face became a deeper shade of violet.

'How fascinating.' Tamara fixed her blue gaze on him.

'We believe in regeneration. The revival of western civilisation.' His voice sounded like that of a man who had often used the words before; he knew them off by heart. 'Values, our example to the world, the fight against barbarism. A renaissance, that's what our allegiance to the Once and Future King symbolises.'

'But does Arthur's Castle have any connection with the story other than its name?'

'Of course it does.'

Sir Hubert Blair said, 'It is true that Tintagel itself, down the coast, is the traditional centre. But that is not to say that this natural stronghold was not at one time used for his purposes. In fact, it must have been, given its position.'

'Perhaps,' Tamara suggested, 'the idea is more important than the precise detail.'

'The details don't matter. Who cares?' the Count interrupted.

'It is a spiritual truth, as much as a scientific one,' Hubert Blair said quickly.

'But there isn't any evidence for the historical existence of a King Arthur,' Tamara said.

'Ah well, that's blasphemy here,' Sir Hubert said. A double first in Greats at Oxford had presumably been the result of an education that discouraged baseless credulity, and a faintly pink tinge spread over his disciplined features.

'I really don't understand about the Grail Foundation at all,' Tamara said.

'It's a tax loss,' Count Kowalski growled.

'It's a charity,' Hubert Blair said.

'It represents a hope for the future,' Lord Collin said loudly. 'It is a chance for men of goodwill to come together for the public benefit.'

'Do you fund a lot of research like Alastair's?' Tamara asked.

'Where we have interests.'

'In medical research, you mean?'

'He means money,' Count Kowalski said.

'Does the Foundation have financial interests in Brazil?' Tamara asked.

'Interests?' Lord Collin shouted. 'You've got it wrong, lass. What we're interested in is what King Arthur himself fought for. Making a stand against the barbarian hordes. Keeping the lamp lit. Christianity. Civilisation.'

'In South America?'

'Tell me a place they need it more.' His voice took on the drone of the experienced speechmaker. 'Our god-given mission . . .' He could, so practised was he, have been talking in his sleep. He was interrupted by a general move to leave the table. The doors at the end of the great hall had been opened to the room beyond. Tamara realised that she was expected to withdraw. She was followed soon by all the men. A mercifully un-mediaeval entertainment was provided, in the form of a film preview. Alastair's ordeal was not to take place until the following morning.

Chapter 7

On Sunday morning Merlin Lloyd sat in his eyrie at the top of Arthur's Castle, watching the bank of screens that showed him what was going on. One was blank. The camera's eye behind what looked like a boss on the heavy frame around the looking glass in Queen Guinevere's room had been obstructed. While the guests were at dinner Mrs Griggs had removed the cosmetics bag hooked over the corner of the mirror. When Tamara Hoyland went up to her room she had found it neatly stowed in the clothes press with her other belongings, all in better order than she had left them.

She had glanced at the bedclothes, turned down with her silk pyjamas laid out on them, and looked around the rest of the room with a faint smile. Merlin wondered whether room service was something to which she was unaccustomed. He examined the girl's short, bright hair, and her colourful and elegantly shaped features. His other visitors were rarely a pleasure to watch.

Tamara Hoyland had crossed the room to open the window, and leant out to look at the night view. She had unfastened her belt and thrown it across the room to land on the figured velvet chair. She slid the scarf from her neck. Merlin was leaning forward to see her next move, when the strip of opaque fabric landed across the looking glass. He had turned up the dial and heard silence but it was not the first time that the loudspeakers in the bedside telephones had failed and Merlin did not want Griggs to know that he had tried to observe a guest whose conversation and actions could not be relevant to the Foundation's work. When Griggs came up for the day's briefing in the morning, the screen for Guinevere's Room was turned off. The others showed a variety of morning rituals. Outside the Castle,

Dr Hope and his girl were strolling across the parterre.

'I might step outside later today,' Merlin Lloyd said. He often used expressions likely to embarrass any literal listener, who was aware that stepping was beyond Merlin Lloyd's power.

He turned away from the screens. His chair had tracks, like a miniature tank, and its power drive and complicated suspension system enabled him to get around the uneven surfaces outside the castle without too much discomfort. Merlin thought of himself not as the user but as the prisoner of his conveyance; but then, the original Merlin had eventually been imprisoned too, chained in a cave by his false love; and there was no term to either's sentence.

In 1950 Merlin Lloyd was a typical Aussie; taller and stronger than the Poms, a handsome young man with the sun ingrained in his physique. Just qualified at Cornwall's Camborne School of Mines, he had been interviewed early one morning at the Regent Palace Hotel in London for a job in Malaya. He was offered the post and accepted it immediately, then he went for a swim.

Would he have done so if he had known that there was a polio epidemic at the time, London's last before the introduction of the Salk vaccine? For years he re-lived that day. If he had bothered to read the British papers; if he had not been so confident of his own invulnerability; if he had not arranged to meet a peach of a girl . . . Infantile paralysis, they called it then; the illness was still a scourge, spread, it was supposed, through the water of swimming pools. The girl had seemed less peachy by daylight, and within three days Merlin had what he thought were the symptoms of flu.

Later, when he was being kept alive by an iron lung in St Bartholomew's Hospital, and after that back at home, miserable, unemployed, unemployable, a burden to himself and his family, nostalgia kept him sane.

A fourth-generation Australian, Merlin Lloyd had been taught that Britain was home. Cornwall had felt like it. The School of Mines was an international centre at the time, with students of every nationality and colour. They were foreigners. In this Celtic land, even though it was not the Wales from which his forebears had sailed to Australia, Merlin was at home. He bought a motorbike and travelled around the county. The Land's End, St Michael's Mount, Brown Willy, Carn Brea, Tren Crom, Tintagel, Arthur's Castle, their smell and shape and the feeling of their earth and stones impressed themselves into his open mind. He knew nothing then of history or legend, of literature or language. His pleasure was innocent and ignorant. In the hot, dry atmosphere of the odorous hospital, he tried to summon up the moisture-laden air, the cool winds, that he might never enjoy again.

Later, as mobility returned to at least the upper part of his body, he began to dream and read about the people who had made Cornwall great. Arthur, the Once and Future King; his Knights of the Round Table – and his magician, Lloyd's namesake, the deathless Merlin.

As soon as the medics allowed, Merlin's father sent the private plane to bring him home. A wing of the house outside Melbourne was converted for him, a special staff taken on to care for him, and everything bought and brought in that could conceivably console him.

The sick room filled up with books, maps and picture postcards. Merlin began a scientific collection of topographical illustrations, and as a kind of occupational therapy built himself a three-dimensional map of the relevant part of North Cornwall. He wrote to friends he had made in the county with lists of places and details of which he required photographs. Tintagel and the empty, derelict Arthur's Castle became his pin-ups.

It was years before he fully accepted that he would never walk again. He would only ever go where a chair could. He was ashamed to be seen in it. He shrank from the remorseful pity of his father, who had never known a day's illness in his life, as much as from the unbearable kindness of strangers. Fantasy became his reality. Outside his gilded cage, the world went on without him: the Lloyd fortunes swelled, his mother died, his father prospered. And the vultures gathered.

The Trust was devised to keep them off.

Elwyn Lloyd, a self-made rich man, had at one time made plans for descendants and dynasties. But Merlin would never father children. Elwyn Lloyd's eventual dispositions were designed to protect the only heir he would ever have. When

Merlin transferred himself to the United Kingdom, he copied his father's sensible arrangements.

By then, Merlin was alone again. After some years of trading on the fact that a very rich man can buy what he wants, he had lost all faith in the mercenary females who put themselves in his way. He had invested too deeply in one and after they were married she let him see that it was his wealth she loved, not him. It took Merlin a long time to sell her on, and the experience put him off women ever since. Better to be lonely, he concluded, than to be a dupe, and he taught himself to distrust the motives of those who purported to enjoy his company.

The new Round Table used the terminology of chivalry; but its founder had no expectation of comradeship.

His British agents told Merlin when Arthur's Castle came on the market. They then tried very hard to dissuade him from buying it. But at last he and the Grail Foundation were settled at Arthur's Castle.

Did the King, not dead but sleeping, appreciate what was being done in his name? Was his existence real or symbolic? Merlin Lloyd was never quite sure himself whether he believed that somewhere, somehow, his hero was dreaming of twentieth-century quests, of a modern Grail.

One could see it as nothing more than a figure of speech. Supporting research was not so different, in essence, from searching for the Grail. A quest, an enquiry, a seeking, research – the difference lay more in semantics than anything else. It pleased Merlin Lloyd to use his money and power to enforce archaisms as the price his clients paid for his support.

Merlin had taught himself to write a good Gothic script and these days he used goose quills and made his own ink. A list of the quests so far funded by the Foundation took up several pages of parchment in a leatherbound tome he kept on an elaborately carved lectern.

Doctor Scientiae Alastair Hope's expedition was the latest entry. Merlin had never learnt Latin, but knew enough to get degrees correct. Its results would be described in English. Merlin looked forward eagerly to hearing them.

Chapter 8

Alastair said the interview, booked for mid-morning, reminded him of taking an oral examination. Tamara likened it to a schoolboy summoned into the headmaster's study. Either way, his appearance before the committee, mentioned in the week-end's programme as 'Presentation of Report by Dr A. J. Hope', caused him more anxiety than Tamara thought was warranted.

After breakfast, they went to look around outside. The air was still and moist, and the faded-looking coastline seemed to shade imperceptibly into a grey sea. The flag drooped on its high pole. On the north, the cliff and castle wall made a continuous barrier. Alastair and Tamara strolled down the east side, on a gravel path separated from the drop by a narrow strip of mown grass and a stone parapet.

'All a bit claustrophobic, would you say?' Tamara suggested.

'With this view?' Alastair gestured to the distant horizon, and then in the other direction, where miles of the Cornish coast lay before them.

'It's all too inaccessible. I feel imprisoned.'

'There would certainly be no escape from here.' The walk-way on the other side of the castle was also constricted by the narrowness of the headland. Stone slabs were laid across the backs of stone lions as seats facing the sunset, and a small area had been set out as a knot garden, rather stunted by the salt winds.

'You look round out here while I'm being cross-examined,' Alastair said.

'Gosh, thanks. What a tempting offer.'

'I'd rather do that than go and confess to this lot.'

'You haven't anything to be ashamed of. It wasn't your

fault that Armand Rivière dropped out, or that Robert died.'

'They are going to think they have wasted their money.'

'Surely they never expected a financial return?'

'It was not discussed as part of the deal. But some of the people here . . . that man you sat next to at dinner last night.'

'Lord Collin?'

'He's just a figurehead. Traces of Alzheimers, I thought after dinner. No, I meant Hubert Blair. He's a Director of UVW.'

'Electronics?'

'And pharmaceuticals. Fleury Adams mentioned it when I saw him in London last week. He thought I knew. And Kowalski is on the board of a mineral and mining consortium called Stewarts. They have interests in South America and Robert Waugh mentioned the name. He had some deal going on that trip that I was not supposed to know about.'

'What was he looking for then?'

'I am not certain.'

'Did he find whatever it was?'

'He never mentioned it.'

'There might have been something in his notes.'

'Everything on him was ritually cremated.'

'Oh Alastair, couldn't you have saved his notebook? After all—'

'No way. They would have killed me if I had tried.'

'But you must have noticed what sort of things he was investigating on the trip.'

'By the time he died I had realised that he was up to something I wasn't being told about. He didn't trust me although we were alone together for all that time in the jungle.'

'A forcing ground for friendship,' Tamara said.

'Or hostility. By the time he died I – well, I was sorry, of course. But if he had disappeared in some less drastic and irrevocable fashion I would have cheered, I can tell you. I suppose it was partly my fault, I should have vetted him more carefully before we left. Armand Rivière too. I didn't consider the human aspect sufficiently, I saw them as professionals rather than people.'

'What was Robert like?'

'You know those Scottish faces,' Alastair said.

'Like yours?'

'No, the other kind, oblong, with great heavy jaws, with light eyes, sandy hair, freckled, sun-sensitive skin – Robert went puce if he forgot his hat for half an hour. And that sort of self-righteous smugness that a lot of Scots have.'

'There speaks a Highlander.'

'Only a Scot may criticise another one,' Alastair said.

'All right, I won't ever do it. My own ancestors were Devonian and Russian,' Tamara said.

'Were they? There's still so much I don't know about you.'

'We need weeks in the jungle alone together then. You must have known everything about Robert Waugh.'

'He was not communicative, really, never talked about his feelings or thoughts.'

'He must have been anxious about Louise.'

'Not so as you'd notice. He hardly mentioned her. But then, she wasn't dangerously ill, we weren't really worried. He complained a lot about the travelling. It isn't comfortable, even with a jeep, where there are no roads or even tracks. We had to walk in the end, if you can call it walking. We hacked our way through, really.'

'You haven't told me much about it,' Tamara said. She had wondered why and regretted it but supposed that Alastair wanted to write before talking, so as to preserve the first freshness of his reactions.

'There has been too much else to discuss,' he said, looking away. 'Anyway you must know what it was like from films and books.'

'Journey to the Green Hell, My Voyage up the Amazon, and thrillers galore,' she agreed.

'Green, certainly. Hellish . . . well, sometimes.'

Alastair had not been entirely unsympathetic or surprised when Armand Rivière turned back. The conditions were exactly what the numerous books described, but the authors had all made them sound less intolerable. When it was one's own skin afire with bites from a variety of vicious insects, one's own violent diarrhoea and vomiting, one's own feet aching and blistered and body burnt, flaking, scabbed, unwashed and stinking, the reality was far worse than the imagination of it. A powerful motive was required to force a man onwards in such a state.

'Were you not tempted to turn back?' Tamara said.

'Often. But Robert and I somehow managed to synchronise our moods. When I was in despair he was all for pressing on and when he felt suicidal I found myself in an optimistic phase.'

Tamara picked delicately with her thumbnail at some grey-green lichen on the stone wall. She said, 'What was driving you on? Was it entirely the quest for medical marvels?'

'Mainly yes, honestly,' Alastair said. 'It's been one of my ambitions ever since I started to think about doing medicine, all my training was designed to qualify me for it. After all, Tamara, you were educated to revere the disinterested pursuit of knowledge as much as I was.'

'Of course, and so I do, but I have never suffered for it.'

'I can't deny that other rewards entered my head – and poor Robert's too, if my suspicions about him are correct. He may well have had the carrot of cash dangling in front of him; and he wanted to out-do Louise. He always wanted to be well known, he never made much secret of that.'

'Don't you?' Tamara asked. Alastair's natural pallor took on a pinkish tone, and she went on, 'What's wrong with wanting to have your achievements recognised?'

'Of course I'd like to be rich and famous as much as the next man. It would help a lot. Think of the support I could get for another expedition if I were well known and successful, I could even pay for it myself if I could only make some money.'

'Might you, out of patents?'

'If I find a drug that can be replicated in a lab . . . it's all waiting to be discovered, Tamara, there's so much to find still.'

'Tell me more about the journey.'

It was awe-inspiring to travel in an unknown region. Even on the most detailed maps in existence, those drawn for the United States Air Force, an area nearly the size of Europe was shown as plain white. Uncharted mountain ranges, cliff-faces a quarter of a mile high, gorges, gullies and rivers lay within it. Stupendous swathes of tropical rainforest, unexplored or at least unrecorded, held treasures of information. There were species of life unknown to science; and tribes of people unaffected by the advances of civilisation, living still as their prehistoric ancestors once did.

'You make it sound so romantic,' Tamara murmured.

But romantic it was not. Higher thoughts were banished by the effort to struggle on through the dripping growth and the thick black mud. The heat lay upon unaccustomed skin like a soaking poultice. A moment's inattention might lead the traveller to touch an eight-inch-long centipede with poisonous hairs or one of the countless varieties of spiders with poisonous bites. At night vampire bats sucked on one's toes. Snakes or predators were at home where man was a trespasser. The first law of the jungle was to be armed with knife and gun; and there was little time to admire the giant, rich-coloured flowers when their barbed or poisonous leaves might be fatal to touch.

Most of the life of the forest went on high in the canopy of trees, hidden from humans, but every inch of every tree seemed to be covered with a jumble of green growth. And every blade and frond was a potential danger.

'But you persevered,' Tamara said.

'One does. And I'd go back, too.'

The drawbacks were intellectual memories, accurately recorded in his notes. But like the pains of childbirth, their horror faded in recollection to leave something more joyous, the experience of being freed of the baggage of civilisation, of living somewhere that was unaltered by generations of technical man.

Robert Waugh had been a good companion in one way at least. He was dogged, ready to press on, not exactly ignoring the discomforts, but enduring them in an almost masochistic way. Whatever nature confronted him with he would outface. It was man he could not take.

It was not uncommon for the Indians they met in the jungle to be at once hostile and intensely curious. They touched, poked, pulled, stroked . . . There was one occasion when both men were borne to the ground by a scrum of women, their hard fingers grabbing and pummelling. It was a nightmare moment. Alastair still shuddered to recall the paint and dirt-blackened hands, the swinging breasts and bellies of the women, the spitting, hissing and shouting. Their paint-striped faces, their distorted features, with holes through lips, nostrils, ears and cheeks and discs of shell or plumes of feather decorating or deforming them, were a nightmare come true.

Other people had been indifferent and some friendly. But Robert deplored even those.

Alastair said, 'Robert simply didn't get on with the Indians. He thought they were dirty and smelly – which of course they are. So what, it's their country. But Robert hated the way they touch and feel people, and he was disgusted by their openness.'

'Nakedness, you mean?'

'That, and the way they don't have any of our inhibitions and hang-ups about physical things. And of course, when we spent a night with them, or even met on the journey, I had to do what I could for them. It's expected of outsiders, people travel with pharmacopoeias even if they don't know what to do with their contents. A good many of the conditions would have been untreatable anywhere, even with more time and equipment than I had. But the Indians didn't see why they shouldn't brandish their suppurating wounds or maimed limbs at Robert as well as me.'

'I am not sure that I would have liked that either.'

'Robert was revolted. But he was missionary material. His ancestors worked for Bible societies. He had that God-given certainty that his own way was the only way. I could just see him a hundred years ago, wearing a black coat and stiff collar in the jungle and teaching converts to cover their flesh with Mother Hubbard dresses. And he would probably have told them that their sexual practices were irreligious. Monogamy and the missionary position, that's what Robert would have preached.'

'How he must have hated falling ill among them.'

'He didn't exactly fall ill,' Alastair said. 'He dropped dead. His covenanting ancestors might have said it was a judgement on him.'

Chapter 9

The knights assembled at the Round Table after breakfast. When they came up to Merlin's tower he was, as always, waiting for them. A niche had been fashioned so as to enclose the chair on which he rolled himself backwards into place, so that when others came into the room they would find him in apparent enthronement.

Hubert Blair always behaved as though he had won his knighthood by deeds of chivalry rather than by the usual progress up a civil service career ladder. He bowed and scraped to Merlin, addressing him as Magistre Doctorissime and introducing archaisms into his speech. On his last visit to Arthur's Castle, Merlin had listened in as Blair told Lord Collin how much the old man enjoyed it. 'I have acquired quite a vocabulary of prithees and sithees,' he had explained. 'I sprinkle them around in conversation to keep our host happy.'

The Count was always informal, being the only one of the company who had known Merlin for a long time. Hector Kowalski was acting as a liaison officer in Australia during World War Two when he met Elwyn Lloyd. The glamorous hero, fresh from feats of glory, and the self-made millionaire became friends and did each other some good over the years.

To the Count, Merlin was still a pitiful, sickly boy, a source of grief. Hector Kowalski had prayed at Lourdes for Merlin. Kindness to the disabled was an act of charity, and for the sake of Merlin's father, and of future profit, he cooperated with his obsessions. But there were limits. He didn't go in for any of this folksy story-book stuff.

'Good to see you, Merle,' he said in the easy accent, learnt from an English governess, that made it sound as though he were speaking his native language. He clapped Lloyd on the shoulder with that self-consciously egalitarian good-fellowship that people use to show they know that cripples want to be treated the same as anyone else. 'You're looking good. Actually, you are looking great.'

Merlin Lloyd's face and features were straight from the Welsh valleys. Dark eyes, skin sallow or olive depending on the state of his health, and once dark hair, now bushily silver, could have marked an Italian or a Jew, but back when he was a student Merlin had merged into the Celtic background like the native he felt he was. He smiled at the older man, and thought that it was good to see a face from his past here in this new and old place.

The men sat at the round table. It was a slab of slate from the quarries up the coast at Delabole, polished to an onyx shine, and inlaid with a large silver sword, with gold chasing on it. The seats were made of a silvery metal. They were as uncomfortable as stone benches and Lord Collin had brought himself a cushion, its abstract design in an artificial fabric discordant in the austere circular chamber whose only decoration was the open sea and sky.

On this, the seaward side of the castle, Guyler and Ghosh had been less anxious to preserve the small windows and thick old-fashioned stone. A vast, thick ring of glass had been manufactured in one piece by a firm that specialised in windows for department stores and penthouses. It was delivered to Arthur's Castle and dropped by helicopter into the grooves prepared for it. The wall of photochromatic glass darkened when the sun grew brighter. The room was carpeted with suede leather, and roofed with what looked like the folds of a campaign tent, swathes of blue printed with an astronomically correct arrangement of stars. Hector Kowalski, the tallest of the knights, had reached up to touch it on his first visit and found that it was not silk but some kind of cold, hard and presumably durable substance.

Nobody brought papers to the meeting of the Round Table; the knights had done any necessary reading before they came. No minutes were taken since everything was recorded.

Apologies were presented from Professor Fleury Adams. Major Griggs reported on current guests. Progress was being made by the team from Atlanta who were working on a new bullet-proof fabric, and as a result two minor patents had already been registered in the Foundation's name.

Excavations in Scotland were revealing, as Merlin had been sure they would, that there were no traces of post-Roman, Arthurian occupation at a site recently bought by an American publicity seeker and proclaimed as the original Camelot.

A coded message telephoned through from Ladakh implied that some proof of the existence of a yeti might be brought back by the mountaineer Evelyn Croxford. He had been sent by the Foundation on a quest for the abominable snowman. A discreet agent was investigating the best way to capitalise on what would be a worldwide interest in the discovery.

The diving team working from New Guinea had not yet found the wreck of the *Philomena*, forty-three weeks out of London and carrying newly minted currency when she went down in 1843.

'Finally, we turn to the quest for medicinal drugs in the Brazilian rainforest,' Major Griggs said.

'We going to have the young man up?' Lord Collin asked.

'We might as well,' Sir Hubert Blair said. 'But it doesn't look as though he's got anything to tell us. I gather the whole thing was a dead loss.'

Chapter 10

Ben Oriel was doing early duty at the gatehouse. Big Mac would turn up any minute with his own lunch and Ben's breakfast from the takeaway at Wadebridge. Not much was happening because the knights were upstairs with the old man.

When Louise Waugh got out of the taxi at the gate and paid the driver off, Ben recognised her immediately.

He took no pleasure in it. She looked even worse, less attractive, less feminine, if that was possible, than she had the last time Ben had seen her. That had been in her house at Buriton. She was the Dean of the Faculty at the time, and Ben had gone to make a final appeal for lenience. She had rejected it not so much with scorn as with indifference.

The lack of feeling with which she told him that his university career was over was not just inhumane but inhuman. Half her attention had been on an open book on the table in front of her. When she spoke to Ben, she kept interrupting this most devastating interview of his life by calling out irrelevant instructions to her husband who was cooking lunch in the same room at the time.

She had frizzy curls then. Ben could remember the longing he felt to plunge his hand into them and pull, drag the woman out by her ginger hair and bang her head on the hard ground outside. He had seen a dead body once. At the age of ten he had found a murdered man washed up on the shore near the cottage in South Cornwall where he was staying. Now the woman's hair was short as though it had been shorn by a man's barber. But those were the same cold, pale eyes set in the same fleshy, charmless face.

Ben thought he had stopped caring about university. It was

the kind of thing that matters intensely at the time, but that very soon reveals itself as unimportant in the scheme of life and especially unimportant to a man whose life had been transformed by revelation.

Ben would have said, indeed had frequently said, that he had put his earlier ambitions and disappointments behind him. But the sight of Louise Dench brought it all back.

He, however, evidently meant nothing to her. Even if he had not been in uniform he was sure she would not remember him. To her he had not been a person, he was just a unit on a production line, a reject of the teaching industry.

The woman had turned up uninvited and Ben was tempted to refuse her admittance. But having taken the trouble to overhear much of the previous day's discussions in the castle, he knew what they were about. When Louise Dench, or Waugh, mentioned the Hope Expedition and her own additional information he realised that they would want to hear what she had to say, as, indeed, Ben did himself.

Big Mac came along on his bike at that moment, so Ben decided to take her over himself. He put her into the passenger seat.

'What's the smell?'

Ben pushed the spy slide so that she could peer through into the rear compartment of the windowless van.

'I brought some fish up from Padstow,' he said.

'Disgusting.'

At the beach she said, 'I can't climb those steps. I've got a bad leg. There must be some other way in.'

Ben took her on to the tramway. Even that, which provoked gasps and questions from any normal visitor, did not bring forth any comment. He drove up to the door of the tram shed, set, almost camouflaged, in the rocky cliff face, and she entered the dim shelter without a word, and climbed into the open car.

The underground access to Arthur's Castle had been built with several motives, the most publicised and commendable being to create work for unemployed miners. The real object was to transport coal and other heavy supplies without heaving them up and over in all weathers. It had not originally been designed to transport passengers but, like the smaller tramway in St Michael's Mount, was intended only for freight. Guyler and Ghosh had left some forgotten cubby holes unmodernised, but the main access tunnel through the rock to the castle itself was back in use. The original tram had simply been an open wooden box on iron wheels. Now Ben handed Louise on to a leather seat, and pulled a waterproof canopy, decorated with fleurs-de-lis, over her head. Even Guyler and Ghosh had not been able to eliminate all drips from the long passageway under the rock; nor had they tried to heat it. Ben grudgingly tucked a fur rug around his passenger's lap.

Faint bulbs illuminated artificial stalagmites. Different coloured spotlights were trained on wall paintings of mournful Byzantine-style saints. The tram rolled up the twin rails with regular, hardly perceptible jerks as the racks and pinions engaged. It came to rest at a platform. Crossing it, they came to the more conventional internal lift, but Ben conducted Louise Waugh into the solar. 'Please wait in here, Mrs Waugh.'

'Dr Dench,' she snapped. 'And I could do with a cup of tea.' Ben handed her a copy of a glossy fashion magazine, a sardonic action intended as a mini-insult but received with indifference.

He said, 'I'll see if somebody will bring you one. You may have to wait for a little while.'

When the castle was built, two dozen servants were required to sustain its owners' lives. When, four hundred years before that, the design to which it conformed was modern, it would have taken an army to maintain – literally, since the men would have been employed as much to fight as to serve.

That was one detail of archaic life that Guyler and Ghosh had not reproduced. Their decorations were the mediaeval dream, but their labour-saving devices were a twentieth-century one.

The castle was full of futuristic devices to make housekeeping less trouble. Some worked better than others. The sprinkler system washed down the marble stairs and hallways quite efficiently, and would no doubt put out accidental fires, but unless it was warm weather left an ineradicable chill in the air for hours after it was used. The suction systems built into each room to take dust and dirt away tended to attract any object that weighed under three pounds. The baths and basins had a newly developed coating that prevented scum sticking to them, though one or two guests had mentioned the curiously waxy texture of the surfaces; and the kitchen was equipped with a variety of devices on which patents were pending, but few were ever used because all the food was delivered ready cooked by a firm in Wadebridge. The previous winter, when Merlin Lloyd went back to his place in South Australia and the Griggses to their bungalow on the outskirts of Newquay, Mrs Griggs complained almost as bitterly about the labour entailed by her own 'fitted dream kitchen' as about the damage the summer tenants had done to it.

Ben told Mrs Griggs that the new visitor wanted tea. Then he went past the open doors of the great hall and on upstairs.

It was part of his job to check the various internal security devices. He had been to a refresher course in Plymouth at Safe Sure's expense in the winter. He reckoned he knew everything there was to know about modern eavesdropping, both how to prevent it, and, of much greater practical use, how to do it himself.

Chapter 11

The castle was completely spurious. That much Tamara knew before she came. The achievements of the Victorian stonemasons had been celebrated in Edwardian glossy magazines. Septimus Trestrail's series of pastiche gargoyles had been copied by church restorers all over the world.

But not all the fragmentary signs of prehistoric occupation had been destroyed by modern building. There were traces of a citadel defended by a rock-cut ditch with inner bank, as well as by the unassailable cliffs. No doubt proper fieldwork on the cliff top would show less immediately apparent archaeological evidence, even though the Arthurian associations were certainly nonsense.

Tamara had woken to a calm morning. She could see the wide sea, shading pearly grey into the sky, pleasantly spread out before her, even without raising her head from the pillow. She thought that it must be like sleeping in a lighthouse, and could understand what had brought generations of the original owners back to the castle for cold and uncomfortable holidays.

But Merlin Lloyd and his Grail Foundation were another matter. She wondered to what extent the worldly men she had met at dinner the previous evening went along with the notion of Arthurian chivalry, and guessed that their motives were far more practical than they admitted. The Lloyd fortune might not be quite in the Rockefeller or Guggenheim league, but it was enough to attract predators; enough to represent a force in itself. Just as mediaeval monarchs needed to know where the mercenaries were, so modern states had to keep track of the wealth that was the contemporary weapon. Tamara understood why Mr Black had been interested in the Grail

Foundation. She had not yet decided what to tell him – if anything.

Tamara remained out of doors when Alastair went in to await his ordeal. Even if she was not here as Mr Black's emissary, she could use the opportunity for her real, her admitted and her lasting profession.

She walked along, her eyes flicking from the ground to the walls, tracing the development of the building and the land use as best she could by sight alone. The weather was roughening. The sea that had murmured pleasantly far below began to hammer against the base of the rock like a thwarted besieger. Wisps of blue-black cloud scudded against a paler grey sky, though it was not raining yet.

Tamara made the most of a chance that might not come again, as she had in the small hours of last night, when she had tiptoed around the castle, listening to snores through the bedroom doors, each with its evocative, chivalrous name. Later, sitting on her bed, she had sketched what she could remember. The prohibition on cameras was a great inconvenience. She was surprised at herself for having obeyed it and already regretted the inadequacy of the records she could keep.

There was not much more she could do in the immediate environs of the castle. Tamara set off towards the steps. The uncultivated slope of the hillside must be covered with traces of earlier inhabitation, but in such heavy rain as now began to fall she would not be able to see much of them. Later in the day, perhaps, she and Alastair could go out together with a tape measure.

A van was coming down the track towards the sea. The driver was the better looking of the security guards, his passenger a woman in a dun-coloured anorak and dark glasses. Tamara watched from above as they drove across the shingle and apparently straight into the cliff-face. Alastair would probably be drummed out of the regiment of Arthur's Castle's beneficiaries if his Significant Other trespassed into its underground passages but later on, Tamara thought, she would ask to be shown them.

Going in, she heard the new arrival talking as she approached the screen that blocked the solar off from the cross passage. The voice was at once harsh and hoarse, its accent more markedly northern than usual.

'You aren't going to get away with keeping the Waughs out of this, Alastair,' the woman's voice said. 'Don't think you can keep the credit for yourself, or the money either. I know what you found in the forest.'

Lousie Dench, Tamara thought, and could not make up her mind whether Alastair would want her to come in.

Peering through the gap in the leather screen, she saw Alastair walk across to the fireplace and perch on the leather-topped fender. He had changed into a dark blue suit, with a blue and white striped shirt, highly polished black shoes, and the tie of the Cambridge University fencing team. I never knew he fenced, Tamara thought.

Alastair, long and narrow, pale and dark, looked not unlike the portrait of St George hanging above the high chimney-piece. The hero was in a shining breastplate, his curiously naked-seeming face and neck emerging from a heavy metal collar. Beside him a dead dragon lay and a living maiden languished, with tears on her cheeks and pearls round her throat.

'Not very appropriate for you, Alastair,' Louise said, 'sitting under the picture of a verray parfit gentil knight.'

Tamara walked into the room. 'Why not?' she said.

'Who are you?'

'We met before, at Thea Crawford's house in Buriton. I'm Tamara Hoyland.'

'Tamara, I think Louise wants to talk to me on our own.'

'Oh, sorry. I'll see you later when—'

'No. Stay. You might as well hear this,' Louise said.

'What's up, Louise?' Alastair said. 'What have I done?'

'You've lied. You have cheated me. You cheated Robert. He's probably lied to you, Tamara Hoyland, unless you are in this with him too. And now he'd lie to the people who put their money into it if I let him get away with it.'

'I don't know what you are talking about,' Alastair said. But he knew; Tamara saw that he knew.

'With Robert dead, you thought you were quite safe, keeping quiet about what the two of you found, saving the credit for yourself. You are stealing his reputation from a dead man.'

'But, Louise, we didn't find anything. You know that as well as I do. You were there yourself.'

'I know as well as you do that when you and Robert went off into the jungle, leaving me behind—'

'What else could we do?'

'All I had wrong was a sore on my leg.'

'You were seriously ill. Your regular medication makes lesions slow to heal, the blood doesn't clot readily, you—'

'All right, maybe I was ill. So you left me behind. And Robert never came back. I find myself wondering quite how he died. Did somebody have a hand in it?'

Alastair said, 'Robert died very suddenly, Louise, there was nothing anyone could do. I know it's hard for you to—'

'Funny that there was someone right beside him who was very much interested in keeping his discoveries to himself.'

'What are you saying?' Tamara asked.

'She is accusing me of being a murderer or a liar. Or both.' Alastair's voice was unmoved, as passionless as though he were speaking to a patient.

'That's as may be. I don't want to end up paying libel damages. But these photos are something else.' Louise flicked the stack of glossy prints so that they fell like fanned playing cards across the marble table.

Alastair moved across the room to look at the photographs which Tamara had already been shown by Thea Crawford. She watched him push them apart with his long, crooked fingers.

'They are the pictures that Robert took after you and he had gone off together,' Louise said. 'I found the films in his backpack. Thea Crawford's seen them, and the lecturer in anthropology. You should have searched his bags.'

'What do you think I am?' Alastair snapped.

'I think you are a man who is determined to get the benefit of this discovery on his own. You weren't even going to tell your paymasters about it, let alone the outside world. There's money in this, not just reputation.'

'I don't know what those photographs are, Louise, or where you got them from, but Robert and I discovered nothing that was not already known.'

'Known to whom?' Louise demanded. 'Look at these pictures,

Tamara Hoyland. Come on, come over here. Look. What are these, then? Who do you think these people are, this child with the stripes painted on his face, or this old man with the lip disk and nose quills? What are the tools they are holding? This is an unknown tribe. It's an unknown place, a lost city. Nobody has ever published anything like them. I've checked. I've spoken to experts. What is the symbol that appears on the old man's chest and on the rock carving he's posing beside? Where were you and Robert, Alastair? What did you find, and whom, and why have you said nothing about it?'

'I have never denied that we made contact with tribespeople in the forest. We lived with them, became friends . . . it was while we were with them that Robert died. You know all this, Louise.'

'You only told me part of the story. You implied that the people you were with were relatively modern and integrated into society. According to my expert in anthropology, these are pictures of an unrecognised tribe. He says they aren't pacified Indians, they are strangers to civilisation.'

'Civilisation,' Alastair repeated. 'Is that what the Indians who leave the forest come to? If these were Indians who had not been in contact with outsiders, forest people who have managed to stay in the forest undisturbed so far, I'm not saying they are, but if it were so, shouldn't they be left alone? It's civilisation that boasted of hunting them down, of killing two million of them in a few decades—'

'You are talking about a different century,' Louise said.

'What makes you think the world has changed? Modern society still destroys their customs, steals their land, kills them in the camps and missions, changes their diet, degrades them . . . that's civilisation?'

'Without it they have a life expectancy of thirty-two. Their infants die. Their children starve. And what art or literature or culture do your precious, unspoilt, native Indians have?' Louise demanded.

'Don't you think that we need the folk wisdom of the few people who still live without artifice? It is what we were paid to go and investigate, as you may remember, and that was precisely because they are the last people on earth who live close to nature,' Alastair said.

'Nature! That's what kills women in childbirth. Only a man could be so sentimental. Give any tribal woman the chance of babies that survive and a washing machine and she'd leap at it, as they all do, when they actually join the twentieth century. Who do you think you are to deprive them of it?'

Alastair moved to the chair by the hearth and sat down. He looked furtive. Tamara turned her eyes away from him. This is disgusting, she thought.

Louise went on, 'Your precious people can do with a good dose of modern artifice, if you ask me. And if they are living on top of El Dorado that's exactly what is in store for them.'

Tamara said, 'I think I shall leave the two of you to—'

'No. Stay. Please stay. I want you to hear this.' Alastair's voice steadied as he spoke. 'I will go through it again, Louise, to make it absolutely clear. Robert and I stayed with a tribe of Indians who called themselves, simply, People.'

'They must have another name.'

Tamara said, 'I believe the people on the border of Brazil and Venezuela, the Yanomani, call themselves by their language's word for "humanity".'

'You must have been doing some research on them, I wonder why,' Louise said.

'After Alastair left I did start reading about where he was going, yes,' Tamara said.

'All right, so he went off to these people . . .'

Alastair went on, 'They were kind and—'

'These are the kind people who let my husband die, I take it.'

'There was nothing they could do. I've told you that before. He died too quickly for anyone to save him. I'm a doctor myself and I—'

'Did you try?'

'As I explained,' he went on, 'these tribespeople were simple and in many ways primitive. But they told us no secrets, and we found no treasures. End of story.'

'I can hardly believe that you're persisting in denying everything. You must be desperate to keep everything for yourself. All that fine talk about searching for drugs and helping humanity – as soon as you see the chance to make your fortune your principles disappear.'

'I don't want to make my fortune and the Foundation is going to lose money on us,' Alastair said. 'There is no Lost City. Those photos can't have been taken on our journey. You can't prove otherwise, Louise. You can't imagine that those canny old men upstairs are going to take any notice of you? I am the one who was actually there.'

'I don't actually care if they would or not. I came on some kind of stupid impulse, I thought I'd give you a chance to tell the whole story.'

'I have. I am. I shall,' Alastair said through clenched teeth.

'I don't know if this lot is Colonel Fawcett's El Dorado.' Louise swept the pictures together and shoved them into her bag. 'It doesn't matter what it's called. All I know is that someone is going to get rich and famous and I'm going to make damned sure you aren't the only one.'

'What are you going to do?' Tamara said.

'What do academics do? I'm going to publish, of course.'

'You bloody well aren't.'

It was the first time that Tamara had seen Alastair lose his temper, or even his self-control. His normally pale face was suffused with a dark, painful flush. A vein in his temple throbbed visibly. His lips drew back over his teeth.

'Alastair, no, don't—'

'You keep out of this.' He shook Tamara's hand from his arm. 'Listen here, Louise, if you imagine—'

'The Knights are ready to see you now, Dr Hope.'

Alastair stiffened at the sound of Major Griggs's voice. His hands dropped to his side, fists clenched. He took a couple of deep breaths, straightened his tie and walked, without a glance at either woman, out of the room.

Chapter 12

When Tamara came downstairs with her hastily packed case, Louise Dench was speaking angrily on the telephone. 'What do you mean, two hours? There must be a taxi available sooner than that . . . oh very well. I'll be at the gate on the main road. Make it sooner if you can.'

'Two hours wait for a cab?' Tamara said in dismay. 'I wanted one too.'

'Apparently they are all off taking people to Falmouth for some reason.'

'I wish I had come in my own car,' Tamara said.

'I might as well telephone from here. I know a chap on the *Telegraph* who'd be interested.' Louise dialled the number for directory enquiries.

'I thought you came to speak to the Foundation Trustees,' Tamara said.

'Not much point if Alastair's sticking to his story. Anyway, I have come to the conclusion that the story should be publicised.'

Ben Oriel came into the room. 'I am going off duty now. Anything you want first?' he said.

'Where are you going?' Louise said.

'Buriton.'

'Give me a lift, can you? There don't seem to be any cabs left in Cornwall.'

'I know, everyone is going to Falmouth to see the trans-Atlantic oarsman come in. I suppose I could take you to Buriton if you want.'

'Have you got room for me too?' Tamara said.

'Sure, why not?'

He stood aside for the two women to precede him out of the door. Louise took her quilted anorak from a row of coats hanging on antler pegs inside the front door, and he hitched his waterproof waxed jacket over his shoulders. The passage past the lift was decorated with glossy trompe-l'oeil murals of armoured men holding blazing torches to light the way towards a platform on which a little carriage was standing.

'Where on earth are we?' Tamara said.

'In earth, not on. This is the tramway, it runs at an angle through the rock to the beach.'

'Just the one shaft?'

'Except for some false starts, the odd side tunnel leading nowhere,' Ben said.

'Is the tramway as old as the castle?' Tamara asked.

'It's just been refurbished, when the castle was restored. It had been blocked up before that. There was an accident during the first war, when the tethers gave way and the whole thing shot downwards and out on to the beach. It was disused and walled off for years. And then when they opened it up to get the thing going again they found it all perfectly workable.'

'Are you sure it's quite safe now?' Louise asked. 'I could somehow manage to walk down if—' The journey up had obviously shaken her more than she had demonstrated at the time.

'All the safety people passed it. You needn't worry. I come and check it every day,' Ben Oriel said.

They moved at an angle downwards through the bedrock, jerking very slightly. There was a slight groan from the machinery.

'It sounds like the trams in continental cities,' Tamara said.

'It is a tram, really,' Ben said. 'It works on electricity, and there's a rack and pinion system.'

'What, dating from the last century?'

'No, it used to be just brute force and gravity.'

The tracks ended in buffers at what looked like the mouth of a cave. The dirty blue van was standing there, and Ben Oriel looked dubiously at his two passengers. 'The back isn't very comfortable.'

'I don't mind,' Tamara said. She climbed over some sacks

and ropes, breathing through her mouth to minimise the smell of fish.

The van bumped up the hill.

I'm running away, Tamara thought. It seemed the only thing to do. Louise had revealed a man she did not know. She had to get away.

Alastair had been abroad, inaccessible and out of communication, for endless months after that happy first week of their acquaintance when they had met every day.

When he came back they both took their new but by now old relationship for granted. After years of independent life, or life dependent on the wrong mate, neither doubted that the other was the right person. It was beyond rational analysis.

With Ian Barnes, to whom Tamara would have been married long ago, if he had lived, there had always been areas of reserve. Tamara disapproved of his profession and distrusted some of his actions in the course of it. She was never entirely sure that she approved of herself for following him into the same work after his death. The indefensible necessities he accepted had to become her own. Some scruples had to be set aside. Some means justified some ends.

That was why, in the end, and before she met Alastair, she had got out.

Before she met him; met him, and the late Robert Waugh, and this woman now sitting in front of her in the passenger seat of Ben Oriel's van.

If only Louise had kept quiet, she thought, then I need never have known.

Tamara had kept things from Alastair too. She meant to tell him about Department E when it was old history. He would see her in a different light, and perhaps find that a waning affection would revive . . . except that Tamara, who once supposed herself the least romantic of women, had actually believed that they would love each other until death did them part.

Instead, and soon, deceit had parted them. Tamara had to get away from him. Her own deferment of her story was forgivable, she believed, because it was no longer relevant. They had not exchanged lists of previous lovers either. But for Alastair to keep quiet about the most important thing that had happened since they met one another was not reticence. It was mendacity.

The man that Tamara supposed Alastair Hope to be would not have pretended that he had come away from Brazil empty-handed, when he had found a lost city and an unknown tribe. Whoever else he kept it from, from whatever motive, he should have told Tamara.

The van was turning past the gatehouse. The driver leant out and said, 'I'll be off then. See you tomorrow.'

'OK, Ben. Have fun.'

'I know you,' Louise Dench, said sharply. 'Were you at Buriton?'

'Yeah.'

'Were you one of my students?'

'I did one of your husband's options. You were the Dean.'

'What's your name?'

'Ben Oriel.'

'Oh. I remember.'

'She sent me down,' Ben said over his shoulder to Tamara.

'Bad luck.'

'I was studying ecology. The environment. Conservation.'

Tamara knew the language. 'You were saving the world?'

'Right.'

'How do you square that with working at Arthur's Castle?' Louise said.

'That's what the Grail Foundation's for.'

'King Arthur and all that stuff?' Louise said disdainfully. 'Dr Hoyland here can tell you what nonsense all that is. She is some kind of historian, I believe.'

Tamara did not feel up to going into the arguments. She said, 'I don't suppose it does any harm to believe in it, if it makes people happy.'

'Just like old times, eh, Dr Dench?' Ben said in an impudent voice. 'People who think they know it all getting it wrong. People like you *would* need material evidence. I pity people who don't have the power of belief.'

'You never acquired that at the University of Buriton,' Tamara said.

'My teacher is a man called Justinian. He has true knowledge, he has got the Third Eye, not that you would understand any of that.'

'Is he down here in Cornwall too?'

'Of course. This is a centre for people who do understand. But they aren't part of your society.'

'I envy you the capacity for faith,' Tamara said sincerely. 'What has Justinian taught you to believe in?' But Ben's intellectually soggy credo was a fashionable cult of unreason. It was not enough to keep Tamara's mind off her own troubles. He rabbited on about the one-ness of the universe and the ancient knowledge of simple people and the energies of ley lines while his two passengers hunched gloomily over their own preoccupations.

They drove along the spine of Cornwall in the pouring rain. Ben stopped for petrol outside Camborne. After what felt like a very long journey they reached the turning off to Buriton, the westernmost town on the south coast of the country.

Louise gave directions to her house. She said, 'If you could see it there's a wonderful view.'

'I know. I've been here before,' Tamara said.

'Are you going to the Crawfords' again?'

Thea was not expecting Tamara. She had come on the off chance, because there was a lift in this direction and because she did not want to go home, where her parents had been expecting her to come with Alastair. She dreaded their kindness.

'I suppose so,' she said.

Louise slid the passenger door back and climbed awkwardly down from the van. In the driving rain, the suburban street was empty, without even any Sunday car cleaners at work. 'I won't ask you in,' she said. 'I must get warm and dry, and then I have some telephoning to do.'

Ben Oriel pulled away from the kerb, splashing water from a deep puddle over Louise. 'I'll drop you near the university if you like,' he said to Tamara. 'I know the way.'

Chapter 13

Alastair Hope told the Knights of the Round Table about meeting the Indians. 'You lay out gifts at a clearing in the forest, little things like mirrors or beads. I took some fish-hooks and penknives. And then you get out of the way and wait. If they take the trinkets you do it again, and it can go on repeatedly, for ages. But if all goes well the people come out in the end and make friends.'

Major Griggs came in to put a note in front of Merlin Lloyd, who glanced at it, looked up at Alastair, and said softly, 'That's very interesting.'

'How did you know what to do?' Jack Collin enquired.

'It's a well-known technique. They call it pacification. You see, the thing is that the indigenous people don't like outsiders to set eyes on them. They see us, one often has the sensation of being observed from the very moment of stepping into the forest, but showing themselves is a different matter. Sometimes it takes years. The Parakanan people resisted every lure for half a century.'

'You succeeded more quickly, I take it?' Merlin Lloyd said.

'I met some of the tribal inhabitants, yes.'

'Leaving aside any unexpected discoveries, Dr Hope, is the Quest Foundation to take it that you found any of the medical remedies you had gone to seek?' Sir Hubert Blair asked.

'Not as yet.'

'I have a note here of the kind of thing we hoped for. You told us, let me see, that the Kayopo people make medicinal use of ninety percent of the plants they have access to. You said that they distinguish between nearly two hundred and fifty varieties of dysentery and have a cure for each; that they have tested methods for controlling parasites by attracting their predators; that they keep strict controls over the genetic types of plants that they cultivate.'

'This is all well documented, Sir Hubert,' Alastair said.

'Your intention was to make further enquiries into materials and methods. You told us that what you could offer was a different technique for gathering information. You said that too many scientists ask predetermined questions. You intended to go with an open mind, listen to what the Indians said and benefit from their native wisdom.'

'I did warn you before I went that there would not be quick results.'

'We hoped for something, however,' Sir Hubert Blair said.

'Even,' Merlin said, 'information that was not in the original brief. There are other exciting things to find in the rainforest, as well as medicines.'

Alastair said, 'This work could take a lifetime. What I have for you at this stage is hardly even a progress report. I can't say any more than that the work has begun. After all, in the eighteenth century Joseph de Jussieu spent thirty years in the forest studying and collecting, just living among the Indians.'

'What good did that do anyone?' Count Kowalski asked.

'Not much in the short term. He was collecting specimens of cinchona, the fever-bark tree.'

'Quinine?'

'Exactly.'

'I thought,' Hubert Blair said, 'that it was one of Von Humboldt's numerous triumphs.'

'He was the first to publish a proper study of the varieties of cinchona. That was at the beginning of the last century. But you see what I mean about all this being part of a long-term study. You have to take the long view. Indeed, before I set off I was promised that the Grail Foundation was prepared to do so. I remember we mentioned Professor Schultes of Harvard who has spent a lifetime collecting.'

'An American,' Lord Collin rumbled.

'Certainly,' Alastair agreed. 'He has found more than a thousand plants that the Amazon Indians use medicinally.'

'Contraceptives, aren't they?' said the Count.

'Possibly a few of them are, sir, yes.'

'You're talking big money there.'

'I imagine the hope of financial reward must have been included in your motives for generously funding my expedition.'

'A bet we lost, eh?' Lord Collin said sharply.

'Only if you expected immediate results. I thought it was accepted that the first expedition could only be exploratory, a preliminary to others, to more detailed study of particular areas. I was under the impression,' Alastair said stiffly, 'that you agreed that at the outset. Am I to understand that the Quest Foundation wishes to withdraw from this commitment?'

Merlin Lloyd fixed his dark eyes on the younger man. 'One of the things we expect in return for backing our young adventurers,' he said, 'is full discussion and frank disclosure. It is what insurers call the utmost good faith.' His voice was deep, musical, as though it had been trained in a male voice choir.

'And the profits are ours,' Kowalski said.

'You surrendered any financial interest,' Lord Collin said.

'That is part of our contractual agreement, as you say.' Alastair agreed.

'Then why is it,' Merlin Lloyd went on, for a moment as awesome as his mythical namesake, 'that you have not mentioned finding El Dorado?'

Chapter 14

Thea Crawford's detached lack of emotion and her lack of curiosity at Tamara's unexpected arrival were therapeutic.

I suppose I am being unreasonable, Tamara thought, pacing the small room while Thea worked.

I don't mention Department E, Alastair never mentioned El Dorado. Shouldn't one cancel the other out? But she felt that he had cheated her.

Late in the afternoon she went out in the mild, moist air and tried to walk off her depression. Trudging under the dripping trees of the arboretum in whose grounds the University of Buriton had been planted, she gave herself pep-talks about having sense and not sensibility; about shelving pride and prejudice. She remembered Alastair when she had first met him at dinner in this town, and later, after he had become part of her life. She felt a wave of affection and remorse.

The university library closed early on Sundays and as dusk fell industrious students began to straggle out of it, books and bags clasped in their arms. Tamara watched them morosely. It felt like a lifetime since she had been an undergraduate at Edinburgh University. How worried the young students looked. How little they had to worry them, in comparison with the buffets and blows to come in the next ten years. The proportion of mature students was much larger than it used to be; they all looked happy and absorbed. There was one who could not be a day under seventy, loading her files and books into the wicker basket of a sit-up-and-beg bicycle; there a stout man in his thirties in leather. He looked familiar, but was one of a uniform type. There was a man in the clothes of a managing director chatting matily with two teenagers in street gear. There, asking a question and being answered with negatively shaking heads, was . . . but Tamara knew him. It was Count Kowalski. She watched as he neatly chose and took a girl from the group, and with her on his arm, his upright figure, dressed in a cavalry-style macintosh, conker-bright shoes steady on the slippery path, strode down the hill and into an expensive, ostentatious car.

Tamara went back to Thea's house.

'Did you say you had seen Louise Waugh?' Thea said. 'I was thinking of calling on her this evening. Do you want to come?'

'Awful woman. I can't stand her. I'll drive over to keep you company but I won't come in.'

They planned the evening ahead. They would order a Chinese take-away on the way out, collect it on the way back. They might hire the video of a costume drama, a genre for which both women had an embarrassing weakness, and drink quite a lot of the excellent wine that Sylvester Crawford collected. Thea, who had finished her article, would make astringent remarks in her beautiful voice and discuss impersonalities. It would all be very soothing. In the morning Tamara would go back to North Cornwall, pick up Alastair and make it up with him. She would explain that she had over-reacted. He would tell her what Louise Waugh had been on about and explain away the photos of the unknown city. She would take him on to meet her parents.

Then they found Louise Waugh's body.

Tamara Hoyland had seen bodies before. She was not immune to blood but could cope with it. She had dealt with worse in her time. Cool, resourceful, efficient; she knew what adjectives appeared in the file that would stay for ever in the confidential section of the Civil Service archives.

So it was not the violent death in itself that shocked her into a kind of incapability.

If the woman had lain down on her bed and slashed her own wrists, as at first sight it appeared, Tamara would have been perfectly calm.

But then there would have been blood in the bedroom and nowhere else.

The bloodstain on Thea's hand had come from the banister rail. That meant that somebody else had been beside the dying or dead woman. Somebody else had either killed her, or left her to die.

Why did the thought of Alastair leap into Tamara's mind? Why did she have that dreadful, completely detailed vision of him tiptoeing barefoot up the stairs, kitchen knife in his hand, and drawing its blade across the drugged woman's arms?

From the moment that Thea implied foul play, the thought filled Tamara's mind.

But if the woman was murdered it could have been done by any of the island's fifty million inhabitants. Tamara's horror was as much at her own capacity for disloyal and untrusting thoughts, as at the notion that they were based on fact. Alastair might have a motive for keeping Louise Waugh quiet, but that was no reason in itself to spring to the conclusion that he had done so. No reason in itself.

Crouched shivering over Thea's fire, Tamara recognised what her eyes had already registered.

A scarf had been lying on the table in the downstairs room. Tamara's eyes had fallen on it again when she entered the house. It was coral-coloured silk, not much larger than a man's handkerchief, crumpled up as though it had been in a pocket. It was not unique. There were other pieces of silk in the world, others exactly that colour and texture, other scarves signed by the same famous Italian designer. But that one was exactly like the scarf, belonging to Tamara, with which Alastair had wiped his car window the day before, and which he had then replaced in the pocket of his coat.

There are none so blind as those who will not see. Tamara, usually so sharp, took no conscious notice of it, but the intuition which is based on unconscious observation of minuscule clues and indications had told her what the brain refused to deduce.

The two women had been asked to return to Thea's house and wait there until somebody came to take statements. It was dark when they got back, and the break in the weather had been refilled by another bank of clouds bringing heavy rain. Wet, shivering and miserable, they scurried indoors. Thea automatically performed as hostess and housewife and drew curtains, switched on fires and poured drinks. Tamara, not distracted in this house by the powerful ingrained habit of hospitality which might have driven her into healing action in her own flat, knelt in front of the hearth, hunched over her knees, her body shaking with long, slow convulsions. She could hardly hold the glass.

Thea Crawford, not naturally maternal or nurturing, had been in charge of students for long enough to let the younger woman's needs take precedence over her own. She was sharp and firm, and very soon Tamara brought herself under control.

Providing and sharing the hot and alcoholic drinks soothed Thea as much as Tamara. Shock gave way to a dispassionate assessment. It was not as though either woman had personal cause to mourn Louise Waugh. Thea had once been the horrified witness to a road accident, and been surprised how quickly she was able to rise above an experience that every motorist dreads. Less likely herself to die with cut wrists in her locked house than to be a traffic victim, she was soon able to think about it calmly.

'I'd have thought Louise was the last person to take her own life,' Thea said. 'Here, have some more of this.'

'Thank you.'

'She was looking for a new job. I had the feeling that she was not entirely sorry to be free from Robert. She was full of plans and confidence when I saw her at the university the other day. I can't understand it.'

Louise had been full of plans and confidence that very morning; on her way to sell a story to the national press, to cash in on Robert's supposed discovery, to get her own back on Alastair. She had been afraid of the tramway. She could walk down if it was dangerous, she had said. That did not sound like a person going home to die.

'One never knows with suicide. They say it's unpredictable,' Tamara said.

'I wonder whether you should ring your father before the police turn up.'

Tamara's father was a solicitor. She said, 'Do you think we need a lawyer?'

'I don't really see why we should, but one can never be sure. I could get hold of my own solicitor.'

'I can't see that it's necessary. All we did was find the body.'

'Perhaps,' Thea suggested slyly, 'you ought to ring Tom Black.'

'Perhaps you ought never to have heard of him. How did you, anyway?'

'Something Sylvester said.'

'Would he have mentioned it to Alastair?' Tamara thought that Alastair might have had an excuse for keeping a secret from her, if he suspected her of doing the same thing.

'Never. But Clovis might have picked something up, I suppose.' Thea's son had met Alastair at Cambridge, one a qualified doctor working on pharmacology, the other an undergraduate. They had been members of the same chamber orchestra.

'I think we ought to eat something. Come downstairs and we'll rustle up an omelette.'

The white and turquoise room on the first floor of the house had come, briefly, to seem like a refuge. Thick curtains draping the three floor-to-ceiling windows, the open fire, the gilt wall brackets, the collection of paintings of the St Ives School, created a barrier of civilisation against the shocks of the day. But Thea was right. They needed food. Tamara followed her down the curving stairs, clutching the wrought-iron banisters. If one had some blood on one's hand, and held the rail, like this, or slid the palm along it, then a stain would be left to mark the next person who used its support. But Tamara's hand was clean. She glanced at it and pushed it into her trouser pocket.

The downstairs room had a large mahogany table at the front end of the house and a wall of kitchen equipment at the back. Thea walked quickly across to pull the blinds down over the windows. She poured some anthracite into the copper Pither heater, and moved the pots of hyacinths from the table on to the sideboard.

'I'll lay the table,' Tamara said. Knives, forks, salt, pepper . . . the egg beater made a calming, homely buzz. 'You know those photographs you showed me when we had lunch at Boulestins.'

Thea poured the yellow liquid on to the sizzling butter. 'Yes, Louise produced some theory about Alastair and Robert having found El Dorado.'

'Did you believe her?'

'Not really. There's not much evidence for the city ever

having existed, and even less for it being full of gold. Did Alastair say anything about it?'

'Actually, he didn't.'

'I see,' Thea said, glancing at her friend and not adding, so that's what's wrong with you.

'I think he wants to make sure nobody goes back where he went. He met an unknown tribe of Indians. He's afraid that they will be exploited.'

'Here, open this and pour us both some wine,' Thea said.

'The thing is, would you say that he was right? This cork's stuck.'

'Let me have a go. Right about what?'

'About keeping what he found secret?'

'I know the arguments of course,' Thea said. 'We're supposed to disapprove of the twentieth-century influence on simple, indigenous people. I'm never quite sure about it. I'd hate to live a simple life myself. Anyway I always wonder about conserving some obscure reptile or plant. I rather think that species die and species evolve continuously, and it's simply sentimental to regret it. Things change.'

'But should we be the cause of them changing?' Tamara asked.

'That's like the conundrum in the science fiction books Clovis used to read. Would a time traveller alter the whole course of later history by stepping on an ant or picking a leaf? I remember one where the hero came back to the twentieth century and found that homo sapiens had never evolved at all, because he had infected some prehistoric creature with his germs.'

'You mean, we need not bother, needn't even try to take avoiding action against the extermination of species, the greenhouse effect, the whole hierarchy of horror that doom-watchers prophesy?' Tamara said.

Thea flipped the omelette into a neat semicircle. 'It seems to me that the whole human race will become extinct in due course. It won't just be a tiny obscure tribe that dies out, but the lot of us. But then I think all existing species and humanity itself are really expendable. Something else will come along to take our place.'

'How calm you sound about it all.'

'I can't say that it worries me, though perhaps that's just

because my child is grown up. I'm not biologically programmed to protect any more. To be fair, the people who bang on about the green death are probably as terrified as mediaeval mothers were of the Black Death, or as my generation was about the bomb.'

'You make all conservation sound like a waste of effort.'

'Actually, I'm the wrong person to ask. Sylvester is the one to discuss it with, not me,' Thea said.

'But you must have some opinion about it. Would finding El Dorado outweigh Alastair's determination to keep his precious people from being corrupted? I wish I knew what to think myself,' Tamara said.

Thea put a perfect omelette, faintly brown on the outside, glistening within, down on the table in front of Tamara. 'Food first, then philosophy,' she said. The front door bell rang. 'I'll go. That will be the police, what bad timing.'

Tamara moved across to finish the second half of the omelette. It did not sound like officials at the door.

'Look who has come, this will cheer you up,' Thea said.

Alastair Hope followed her into the room.

Chapter 15

When he could not sleep Merlin Lloyd stopped trying. He put on his dressing gown and set off round the castle and sometimes outside it. He knew perfectly well that what mediaeval man had seen could never be reproduced. Pollution and corruption were inescapable. Even at night, when the worst details of the coastline's ruin were hidden, orange lights cast their artificial colouring on to the sky. Planes landed and took off from RAF St Mawgan and man-made satellites disturbed the stars. Merlin doubted that King Arthur would recognise his country when he revived to save it.

From certain aspects, though, the view must be almost unaltered. On the north side of the castle where the walls rose smoothly from the cliff, its windows looked on to nothing but the sea. Tonight, in rain and wind, there was total blackness, and even through two thicknesses of glass the howl and thunder could be heard sufficiently strongly to give the illusion that the structure itself was shaking.

Merlin took himself down in the lift, and out on to the eastern walkway. He made no attempt to shield himself from the rain. The wind would tear any umbrella from his hands, but he had come out especially for the contact with elemental weather. In his imagination he rode a fiery steed through night and fog, across the moors past sleeping villages, fording rivers, galloping along the hard yellow sand, tirelessly criss-crossing the country in the persona of a knight in shining armour. If he could actually do nothing, in fantasy he might as well do everything.

He scooted the chair along the dark terrace, screwing up his eyes against the driving rain. Alone in the dark, unobserved by anxious care or impatient pity or dignified scorn, he could almost recall the sensation of physical freedom. His swift, silent glide stopped at the low wall separating the plateau from the sheer drop to the noisy sea below.

He was a knight without a squire. Once he had stood on a similar cliff top with a friend, a boy from Nigeria who had been at the School of Mines. Might he have had friends of his own age if he had stayed in the country where he had been a student instead of being taken home to Australia? Might he have found people who were at ease with him, if he had not been so rich and protected? After many years, he was resigned to loneliness. But it would have been nice, he thought, if there were someone who was neither servile nor patronising, to whom he could simply say, 'Look at that!'

Swivelling the chair, he propelled himself forward and up the ramp into the castle. It was necessary to be silent now. His wet hands slipped on the chair's controls. Absurd that he was forced to be careful not to disturb anybody, at his age, in his own house. Such a fuss there would be. A man who was not a man could never with impunity get wet or behave irrationally.

Merlin moved on his silent wheels along the passages and through the downstairs rooms. Guyler and Ghosh had made a wonderful job of them, not realising Merlin's dreams but creating what he would have dreamed if he had had the frame of mind to do so. Dreams, fantasies, eccentricities? He kept Arthur's Castle hidden from outsiders' mockery like the electric train set that his own grandfather had played with in old age. Once Merlin was dead, his gigantic toy would be sold and the Foundation turned to profit-making.

He shrugged his shoulders, indifferent to the familiar thought. The world was coming to an end in any case. It would not long survive him. Who was crazy, the man who accepted the appalling present, or Merlin, who lived in the optimistic past? He went on through the solar and into the hall.

One of the guards was standing by the outer door. He looked appalled at the sight of his employer. 'Night round, sir.'

'In the house?'

'I just came in for a moment out of the rain.'

'For a moment? You've hung your coat up.'

'I didn't want to drip all over everything.' The boy looked sulky, young and one hundred per cent healthy, his damp brown hair springing into corkscrew curls above a pink and pointed face. Merlin felt a pang of hatred. Long ago he had ill-wished other men who were whole. Shocked to have reverted to the pointless malice he had eventually put behind him, he made amends for an offence its victim never felt. Wheeling himself into the lift cage he said, 'You can take me up top.'

'Yessir.' Ben pressed the appropriate button, which was a gold disc carrying the profile of a crowned king. 'Sir, you're dreadfully wet. Should I fetch Major Griggs?'

'Don't fuss. You can come in and pour me a drink.'

Ben had not been into Merlin's private rooms before.

'Over there, on the table. Mine's Scotch. Take one for yourself too.'

The door into the office was half open, and Merlin saw the young man glance at the bank of dark screens.

'Didn't know I could keep an eye on you, did you? No need to look like that, I haven't seen you misbehaving yet. Wait while I get something dry. Stay here.'

When Merlin wheeled himself back, having changed some of his clothes, he found Ben looking at his tapestries. Guyler and Ghosh had acquired them illicitly and exported them from Austria without the proper permits. They were early mediaeval representations of a coronation. An etiolated king sat on a stone chair, holding a gold circlet above his head. Around him knelt a loyal crowd. Behind it a variety of animals, including a unicorn and a griffon, looked on. On a table in front of the throne was a small gold cup on a splayed stand.

'I kid myself that's the Holy Grail,' Merlin said.

'Wasn't it any bigger than that?' Ben asked, disappointed.

'Who knows? If Arthur really was a war leader of the Dark Ages and kept the Roman flame burning against the Anglo-Saxon invaders, then that's what a contemporary chalice would have looked like. Not very exciting by our standards.'

'Is that what King Arthur was?'

'So the scholars say.'

'Scholars!' Ben Oriel said contemptuously. 'Men who think

they know everything and know nothing. But there's none so blind as those that will not see.'

'Sit down.' Merlin pointed to the chair usually used by Major Griggs. 'What do you think we're doing here, boy? Some quaint old mummery?'

'I don't know.'

'No reason why you should. Griggs would say it wasn't your business.'

'I think that this place is my business, Mr Lloyd.'

'How's that?'

'You must know that Arthur's Castle is built upon a site of power. The impulse is one of the strongest in Britain. That's probably because it has not been contaminated by use and development. It is of world-class importance.'

'World class?'

'This isn't the only country affected by lines of force. We are connected by a grid that spans the world.'

Ben began to tell Merlin Lloyd about his beliefs, knowledge and expertise. He spoke of the third eye, and ley lines, and the submerged city of Lyonesse. He mentioned the wisdom of the ancients and the destructive corruption of modern society. He was exalted, and Merlin watched him agnostically, amused at the young man's impertinence, and aware what the prosaic men now asleep below would think of his beliefs.

'Man's future depends, our planet and all its inhabitants depend, on our knowledge of orgone—'

'Orgone?' Merlin Lloyd asked.

'The secrets of life-energy,' Ben explained. He was using the words his friend and teacher Justinian had used to him. 'Man has created a vacuum by being too clever and insufficiently wise. Our technical mastery of science has moved too far ahead of our philosophy. And now the Earth herself holds us responsible. Those of us who can hear and see have to cooperate and share our initiation into the earth-secrets as we make our peace with the unknown.'

Merlin Lloyd was too rich, cynical and scientifically educated to accept uncritically arguments that had been swallowed whole by Ben Oriel. But he did believe that man had broken his age-old truce with the unknown. In establishing his protest against the twentieth century, Merlin had told himself that the Holy Grail, and Arthur and his knights, were no more than symbolic; to those who derided even symbols, he had implied that they were a game. But in the time he had spent at Arthur's Castle he had begun to wonder whether there was more to his allegiance than a cripple's comforter. Merlin had come to distrust a world in which change had become the norm, and in which the pattern of rules that governed humans and their environment was torn and unstable. Science was not enough any more, if it ever had been.

Ben Oriel, well taught, and having always had a capacity for parrot-learning, which, when he was younger and more frivolous, came in useful for taking off the masters at school as well as repeating their words verbatim in exams, was fluent and in a curious way impressive.

'What are you going to do about it? Apart from talking?' Merlin Lloyd asked when Ben finally stopped talking.

'Don't kid yourself that it's all just words. I can fight, you know. People have to learn to respect life.'

'You'll make them respect life if it kills you,' Merlin said, uncharacteristically humorous. He liked the young man. That's what's been wrong with me, he thought, I don't see enough young people, with their principles and enthusiasm still bright. All the usual hangers-on just say what they think I want to hear.

Ben said, 'We shall fight for what is right. It's the only way to stop the big battalions destroying everything that is precious in the world. They have got to be made to conserve endangered peoples, protect threatened species.'

'I always found people the most exciting species. When I was your age I got caught up in the early history of Cornwall. I was here as a student, did you know that? Arthur, Guinevere, Merlin, the Knights of the Round Table . . . King Mark, Tristan, Isolde . . . they took me out of myself. Do you know what I mean?'

'Of course.'

'Most people haven't a clue what I am talking about.'

'Most people are fools.'

'And you have your own grail to seek. The human race

is divided into seekers and the satisfied. All these stories are metaphors for it.'

'The idea of the Quest, you mean?'

'That, yes. The Foundation helps people to go hunting. That's all research is, you know. A kind of hunting. A quest. It's just fancy language for it.'

'And King Arthur. Do you really believe in him?'

'Does it matter, so long as his name is attached to an idea which is still valid? Men need their heroes and martyrs. They need their legends. Aborigines in my own country with their songs, Christians, tribesmen in the Amazon, Texans at the Alamo, the Jews at Masada.'

'So many people try to debunk stories like that. It's as though there's something good about being sceptical. I believe in belief,' Ben Oriel said fiercely and Merlin Lloyd replied,

'We destroy humanity's myths at our peril.'

Chapter 16

'There was something in Louise's house. Something of yours.' Conversation over supper had been halting, and Tamara's remark, uttered almost to her own surprise, broke a long silence.

Alastair's face assumed the non-committal reserve that medical students learn along with their anatomy, and Thea Crawford said, with apparent relief,

'I shall leave you to it. I am going to bed.'

'But the police haven't come yet,' Tamara said.

'I don't expect they will get round to us till tomorrow. Anyway I'm not sitting up all night for them. If there's a knock at midnight I shall complain of harassment to the Chief Constable.' Gathering up two books, the Sunday papers' colour supplements, one of the pots of hyacinths and a glass of whisky and soda, Thea went up the stairs. They heard her through the thin old floorboards of the drawing room overhead as she turned off lights and guarded the fire. Then she went up the second flight to the bedroom floor. 'Goodnight,' she called down. 'See you in the morning.'

'She's left us alone to talk,' Alastair said.

'Not so much from tact as lack of interest,' Tamara said. 'Emotional crises and heart-to-hearts aren't Thea's line.'

'I can see that there is a crisis.'

Tamara gazed at Alastair. He was not the first man in her life since the death of the man with whom she had meant to spend it. Others had come and others had gone. One had been a bad choice; but then, as Tamara had told herself at the time, nobody thought the less of men who temporarily succumbed to beautiful female temptations. On the occasion of a memorably awkward farewell, he told Tamara that she was incapable of faith or trust. Such epithets retain their sting. Now, remembering them, she told herself to trust Alastair.

'What's the matter?' he said. 'This isn't just Louise Waugh's suicide,' he said. 'What is it, Tamara?'

She said, 'The handkerchief. It was in Louise's house.'

'My— ?' Alastair felt in his pockets and drew out one clean and folded white handkerchief and a crumpled, used blue one.

'Pink silk. A scarf actually, it was really mine.'

'It was in my coat pocket. I was wiping the car window with it on the way down.'

'I know.'

'Wait.' He went out of the room, and Tamara heard him opening the front door and going down the steps. Soon he came back, holding the dark-coloured, waxed jacket. 'It should be in . . .' It was not. Not in either of the large side pockets, not in the sleeves, not in the coat at all.

Staying on the far side of the room, watching him warily, Tamara said, 'Is your coat marked?'

'Only by St Michael. It's Marks and Spencers. I must have picked up someone else's by mistake,' Alastair said.

'When?'

'At Arthur's Castle. It was hanging in that lobby by the front door.'

'Were there others like it?'

'I didn't notice.'

'When was that, Alastair?' Tamara's voice was tight with distress and suspicion.

'After I had seen the sponsors and come down to find you'd left. You might have told me. Or at least left a message. I spent most of the day trying to find you.'

'Where?'

'At your parents' to start with.'

'Did you go there?'

'No, I rang your mother but she said you hadn't arrived and anyway they weren't expecting you till tomorrow, so then I went along the coast to Tintagel. I thought you might have gone to do some more fieldwork. I wasted an hour slithering round there in the rain. Then I rang your mother again. I have to tell you that she sounded more amused than anxious. And then I came here, but there was nobody in when I got to this house, so I drove round a bit aimlessly, and then I thought I'd better go back to Arthur's Castle and see if you'd turned up there, and then I drove past Thea's again and saw the lights on . . . and here you were.'

Tamara got up and went across to the kitchen end of the room, gaining time by putting the kettle on. 'Coffee?' she said.

'Tea, please.'

She thought, do I really believe that this man is capable of murder? She said, 'The scarf isn't unique either. It was from Liberty's.'

'Where was it?'

'On the table in Louise Dench's house. I thought you'd killed her. Just for a moment, I actually thought you'd cut her wrists to keep her mouth shut.'

Alastair pushed his chair back, his face blank. 'I'd better go,' he said.

'No, wait.' Should she explain that she was cautious because another lover had once conned her into ignoring the signs of his criminality? But there was nothing in common between the two men, nothing at all, except Tamara herself. 'I'm only telling you this because I can't believe it,' she said. 'Inside me, instinctively, it doesn't feel as though it can be true.'

'You can't base your behaviour on feelings,' he said coldly.

'I can. I have. I do.' Soon she would tell him how doing so had more than once saved her life, and how often, in her experience, objective evidence and proof followed an instantaneous, subjective certainty. 'Alastair, I am ashamed that the idea entered my head. It seemed so plausible, so possible, so utterly awful, that it made me ill. Now I'm sure it isn't true . . . is it?'

'Wouldn't I say that in any case?' he said.

'Never mind. I do believe you. I don't believe it. Sometimes one has to listen to . . . to the heart, even though all my other instincts revolt against the idea that I could be illogical or emotional.'

'And can you be?'

'Apparently. I know, in here – ' Tamara put her hand on her breast, 'I'm sure you couldn't have done anything wrong.'

'There is still a "but", isn't there?'

'But you quarrelled with her this morning. And then, the scarf that you had used as a handkerchief, or at least one like it . . .'

'Very Shakespearean,' he remarked.

'Othello never had the sense to ask Desdemona for an explanation though.'

'I can't explain having a coat that is not mine and not having the handkerchief that is.'

'But you could explain about the lost city. I couldn't believe you would have kept something so important from me, that was why I left Arthur's Castle. It seemed so . . . such a betrayal. Louise was talking about El Dorado. Alastair, I have to ask you. What were the photographs Louise produced?'

'They were of a ruin in the jungle. I suppose it had once been a city, there were stone structures and open spaces, almost swallowed by undergrowth and trees but one could see it. No gold, Tamara, no ornaments, just stones and jungle. I suppose I should have realised what it might mean to other people, to you as an archaeologist, but honestly it hardly registered as important at the time. And it can't have been El Dorado. That was in another part of the wood.'

'I thought nobody knew where it was supposed to be,' Tamara said.

'Of course nobody can be sure, Colonel Fawcett never reappeared and there were no proper traces of him. But nobody believes he went anywhere near the district I was in. Don't start believing in that treasure and gold, I do beg you. It's a will-o'-the-wisp.'

'Whether or no, Alastair, I can't understand why you never mentioned it, if only to me. After all . . .'

'Do you think we have time to talk? Or are the Devon and Cornwall Constabulary about to arrest me?'

'Not through anything I said. Here's your tea.'

They pulled dining chairs close to the stove.

'I wasn't going to tell anyone, not even you,' Alastair said. 'I decided that the only way to keep a secret for ever is by being the only person who ever knows it. And it's so important, I didn't even feel guilty about it. By not putting it into words, I made it not exist.' Tamara slipped down off the chair on to the hearthrug and rested her back against Alastair's knees.

Thea had left her bedroom door a little open. She reclined comfortably in the electric warmth of her large bed, leafing through an article about the Middle Bronze Age in Silesia, with the distant hum of Alastair's deep voice audible two floors below. She was not surprised that the quarrel had been made up, whatever it was about.

'You have to understand what it's like,' Alastair said. 'Many of the native Amerindians have been dispossessed of their land. They are destitute, degraded, starving, sick.'

'Surely there's some protection for them?'

'The Brazilian government has a department called FUNAI, The National Foundation for the American Indians, but the brancos, the whites, win every time. We take their land for mining, hydro-electric schemes, cattle farming, we cut down their trees, drive new roads deep into their homelands. We turn the women into prostitutes and the men into pimps. They become beggars. We destroy their culture and replace it with degradation. I'm sorry, Tamara, I shouldn't preach to you but I feel so strongly . . .'

'I do see Survival International's journal sometimes.'

'Then of course you know all this. And you'll understand why I have to protect the People, whatever the cost.'

Contact with them had come at last when Alastair and Robert were beginning to think they had done all they could for the time being. This was only supposed to be a preliminary visit. They had seen enough to decide what they should do next year.

They were walking along a narrow path that wound through thick jungle. The way was impeded by the curious roots called stilts which grew down from the trunks or branches of high trees, like the spokes of a vast umbrella, and by the woody, contorted lianas growing upwards to seek the light above the forest canopy. From time to time they heard the crack of creaking wood and the muffled thud of a tree falling to the ground when its shallow anchorage gave way. Huge, brilliantly coloured butterflies and parrots flashed across the dark cover of foliage that almost entirely blocked off the sunlight. Snakes slithered silently out of sight; ants carrying emerald green leaves four times their own size marched across the route. Spiders' webs the size of bed sheets dangled across the path.

'We never expected to meet anybody. Then there was this man who appeared in front of us quite suddenly and silently. He was naked. His body was covered with streaks of ashes and he had a bright blue feather through his nose. He was carrying a bow and arrows. We were terrified.'

Robert and Alastair had taken in all the awful warnings about murderous and man-eating natives in the jungle, and it was not easy to interpret the man's gestures.

But the People were friendly. The man conducted them onwards to a village set in a clearing. It consisted of huts made of bamboo poles and palm fronds, very small so that even the natives could hardly stand upright. The visitors were given food, and shown a place to sleep. They were made inexplicably welcome.

'The People had the odd bit of twentieth-century junk around but we saw hardly any signs of contact with the outside world. And they had achieved what seemed to be a perfect symbiosis with their natural habitat. Of course they had some illnesses we have learnt how to cure. Some of the children . . . I couldn't do much for them, I didn't have the equipment. And they could be fierce, too. We realised that when some strange Indians appeared and were driven away quite mercilessly with spears and arrows. We couldn't understand why they had taken us in. We began to get a bit nervous in case they were fattening us up for a feast.'

But Alastair was able to treat some of the children's ailments and the adults' too. He and Robert were taken out with the hunting parties. On one of those excursions they came to the ruins of a great city. The place was simply taken for granted by their hosts, as much part of the landscape as the trees themselves, but they posed for Alastair's polaroid camera beside some of the monuments and accepted the prints with great amusement.

Alastair had not been all that interested in the ruins. 'Sorry, Tamara. Old stones and dead civilisations are a closed book to me.' Perhaps that was why he had not observed that Robert was recording the city. 'What mattered was our relationship with the People.'

When he met the People's grand old woman Alastair discovered why he and Robert had been so well received. She summoned them into her presence. She looked a hundred, but she was probably no more than half that age. To their astonishment she addressed them in halting, ungrammatical but quite understandable English. She had learnt it from another outsider, long long ago when she was a child.

Once upon a time two men had come through the jungle. They visited the People. One man had died quite soon after arriving. The other stayed. He was wise. He was good. He had taught the people things they had not known. He was their father, though only metaphorically, Alastair thought. He could see no physical signs of European genes in the group. In the end the man had gone away. The woman remembered the weeping and wailing when he left. But he had said that he would return. When they needed him, he would be there.

'That was why they welcomed us, Tamara. Returned, reincarnated, revived, they thought we might be that white man come again.'

'Didn't they ever see him again?'

'No, and he must have been ancient when he left. The old woman spoke as though he had stayed for generations. I should think he went away to die, perhaps he even wanted to keep his legend alive.'

'Another Once and Future King?' Tamara suggested.

'I think it must be a universal human dream. The king who comes back to life to rescue you, the resurrection of the saviour. Because, of course, the People didn't know they were living in Paradise already. Their own worries loomed as large to them as ours to us, crops that failed, lovers who didn't love enough, children who didn't thrive, an ever-threatening tribe of barbarians somewhere else in the forest.'

'How soon did they realise that you and Robert were false messiahs?'

'They took a lot of convincing, especially after Robert died, just like the first man's companion had. I think they believed me in the end, when I insisted on leaving them.'

'And do you want to go back?'

'In some ways I do. I think we have a lot to learn from them

– quite apart from the fact that they actually seem to have some remedies that could be useful to us.'

'It sounds as though you were able to reciprocate.'

'Obviously modern surgical methods do cure conditions they are helpless to treat. There was one young woman with a displaced hip joint, and a lot of dental problems, and then . . . well, there's no point in mentioning everything. Of course I could help them if I went back properly equipped. But I am afraid.'

'Of them?'

'No, for them. Any further contact with the outside world would probably destroy their way of life, as it has done for so many other peoples in Amazonia, and if I let the discovery of the lost city be known there certainly would be no saving them. You know what the idea of El Dorado would do.'

'Or any other lost city, not just El Dorado.' Tamara felt a yearning in her own voice. 'I am not immune from the dream myself.'

'Treasure hunting?'

'That too. I can't deny it. But for an archaeologist, think of a whole city . . . but you have to be the one to decide.'

'What do you think, Tamara?'

She pulled herself to her feet. 'More tea? No? I'm terribly thirsty.' She went and stood by the mantelpiece, looking at Alastair's reflection in the big mirror. 'Look, I know the arguments. You could hardly have escaped hearing them over and over again in the last few years. I can see what Louise meant and I have some sympathy for her views too. But then I can understand your attitude just as easily. I can't judge and I don't have to either. It's for you to decide, and now that Louise is dead, only you.'

'I promise you, it's the only way. The alternative is degradation at best, genocide at worst. But I can trust myself not to tell.'

'And me?'

'Of course. Anyway, you don't know where it is.'

'So you have got maps and records then.'

'I did, but I destroyed them. It seemed the only thing to do.'

'And Louise Waugh had the photographs,' Tamara said.

'They must be in her house, unless the police have taken them. Do you think . . . ?'

'Nobody will know what they are. They could be anywhere.'

Tamara put out her hand to pull him up. 'Let's go to bed. I have never been so tired.'

'Can I stay, then?'

'Don't be silly. But Alastair, you can't destroy your memory. You still know where the People are.'

Chapter 17

Count Hector Kowalski and Sir Hubert Blair were experienced campaigners and even if they had not had recent evidence of the intercommunications between the rooms of Arthur's Castle, neither would ever conduct a private discussion indoors, unless the room had been swept for bugs by people they trusted. But it was safe enough on the cliffs, especially in bad weather when natural interference prevented long-distance surveillance or eavesdropping. It would have been natural to shout above the wind. Instead each man pitched his voice low and put his mouth close to the other's ear.

'El Dorado,' the Count murmured in the voice he might have used in wooing.

'A lost city full of treasure,' Sir Hubert said. 'If it's true . . .'

'You heard what Louise Dench said.'

'We both heard Alastair Hope contradict it too.'

'Oh, that city exists all right.' The Count patted his jacket pocket.

'Cigarette?' Hubert Blair asked, producing his own.

The Count took one and held it to the gold lighter. He said, 'My old father used to say that gold would go off. He thought one should invest in uranium instead. But it's better than ever – and then, there's the antiquity value.'

'It will have to be carefully managed. Serious collectors only. We'd never get the stuff out of the country if the Brazilians got a hint of it.'

'Not so easy to hide a whole city,' the Count remarked.

'Only until we have rescued the valuables. After that, of course, they can do what they like.'

They walked side by side, bending forward against the wind,

a few feet in from the cliff top. Neither took any notice of the pounding sea below.

'The question is whether Waugh came up with the rest of the goods,' the Count said.

'Those records of lost cities and lost tribes won't be all,' Sir Hubert agreed. 'UVW was hoping to know of the pharmaceutical implications as soon as possible. Do you think we shall be able to get Hope to talk?'

'Of course,' Count Kowalski said, surprised. 'It's only a question of finding the right carrot or stick.'

The two Knights of the Round Table walked on, one limping, the other stooped, considering how to make the most of the situation. Not many of the Quests Merlin chose to subsidise were capable of generating worthwhile profits. Most were, no doubt, interesting in their own way, but not essentially relevant.

'You don't remember old Lloyd,' Kowalski said.

'Elwyn Lloyd? No, I never met him. What did he think about King Arthur and the rest of it?'

'It was all under control while he was alive,' Kowalski said. 'But I talked to him about it once. He said it didn't do any harm and made Merlin happy. He always felt guilty about the boy, quite unreasonably so. The polio wasn't his fault.'

'In other words, he thought the whole thing was nonsense.'

'He didn't care so long as it kept Merle amused.'

'My sentiments exactly,' said Sir Hubert Blair.

They walked on, their thoughts on parallel tracks. Naturally they looked forward to inheriting the control of the Foundation. It had to be soon, Sir Hubert thought. The best man in Harley Street had confidentially provided the expert opinion that Merlin Lloyd's life expectancy was short.

It would be a relief to be spared the weary journey and the absurd play-acting that kept Merlin sweet. Hubert Blair did sometimes wonder whether his and Kowalski's efforts were properly appreciated by the other board members of their respective companies.

Both UVW and Stewarts already had big interests in Brazil, a land generously endowed with every natural resource, and subject to none of the natural perils such as earthquakes, volcanoes and hurricanes. Sensible western corporations regarded investments there as a stake in the future, but none would sniff at a more immediate return; some of Hubert Blair's colleagues were also highly cultured men for whom the treasures of the past would mean even more than their financial value. None, he assumed, would be carried away by such an emotion. He said, 'It would never do to let Merlin suppose that Dr Dench should be taken seriously. Have you thought of that?'

'He will have to be gently steered in the right direction,' the Count said.

'So you're going to stay on a little longer?'

'The food's bad and I can't stand the climate, but duty calls.'

It began punctually to rain again and the two men took the shortest route into the castle. Merlin was downstairs in his chair.

'Have you been out in this weather?' Kowalski said.

'Just up and down in the tram. I always think the tunnel is Guyler's masterpiece,' Merlin Lloyd replied.

'Of course you are at home underground, with your mining qualification,' Hubert Blair said.

'That's true, certainly. And I am always reminded of my namesake, the original Merlin, carrying the new-born infant Arthur away from his mother, through the rock passages of Tintagel to safety.'

'I don't mind admitting it gives me the creeps down there,' Hubert Blair said, shuddering.

'I can see why,' said the Count. 'A man could be buried alive.'

Chapter 18

The telephone rang at dawn. Thea shouted down the stairs in a voice husky with sleep. 'Alastair. It's for you. Take it in the kitchen.'

When he came back to the bedroom it was to say that he had been summoned back to Arthur's Castle.

'How did they know where to find you?'

'I don't know. Does it matter?'

'What are you going to tell them?'

'I wish I knew.'

'Best tell them nothing at all. Lie at home for someone else's country.'

'Come again?'

'Like ambassadors who tell lies abroad for their own.'

'That's rather what I thought. May I use your toothbrush and razor?'

Alastair set off to return to the north coast while Tamara, who intended to join him later so that they could go on together to her parents, waited to see the police. But by mid-morning Thea was still pacing her floor in ill-controlled impatience.

'I hate being kept waiting,' she said.

'You are simply going through what most women suffer every time someone comes to mend the washing machine,' Tamara told her. But it was a long time since Professor Thea Crawford had suffered a housewife's minor daily irritations. She always solved domestic problems by throwing money at them. Overtime payments for her housekeeper, incentive payments for her tradesmen, private medicine, expensive dentists and a hairdresser whose appeal was to busy clients, preserved Thea from the frustrations of life.

Giving evidence, however, could not be delegated. She paused in the sunny bay window. Gangs of girls walked down the hill in brown dresses and blazers designed half a century earlier to render their wearers unattractive to the opposite sex. Boys in almost equally archaic maroon, undeterred, buzzed around them in ecstasies of display ritual. The refuse wagon ground its way down, the milk float clattered up, the postman pushed his three-wheeled trolley, the commuting traffic from the new housing estates inched forward towards the town centre hooting at the obstructions. Thea hardly even noticed this daily street scene. But there was no sign of a police car. 'Damn it, I am lecturing at eleven.'

'You'll have to cancel.'

'I never cancel my lectures.'

'They always say that's what is wrong with successful professional women. We are over-conscientious.'

'That's how we get to be successful professional women,' Thea said.

'Here's another, Thea. Ten-thirty on the dot.'

'About time too.'

A woman police constable parked her official car where no private motorist could, outside Thea's front door. She was admitted and introduced herself as Sheila Parkin. Had she come earlier, Thea might have tried harder to insist that the blood on her hand should be regarded as important evidence. As it was, she recounted her experience concisely, went over it patiently and left.

'Did you see the blood?' the constable asked Tamara.

'Yes.'

'But you don't know that your friend never touched anything in the room where she found the body.'

'I only went up afterwards, as I told you,' Tamara said.

'So she could have gone in and put her hand on something, maybe touched the body to make sure she was dead. It would have been the natural thing to do. You did it yourself.'

Tamara looked at the young woman; clear, wide eyes, the fresh complexion of someone brought up in an Atlantic climate, the acquired incredulity of her trade, combined with a presumably innate conventionality. This girl has already decided what two women academics are likely to be capable of; and unemotional behaviour when confronted by violent death was not expected.

Tamara opened her mouth, and closed it again. What am I doing, she thought, trying to persuade them that a murder took place? Almost against her will, she offered coffee. 'It's not my own house, of course, but I know my friend would want me to . . . Milk? Sugar?'

'Great, thanks. I could do with that. What a kitchen!'

'Lovely, isn't it? Sylvester Crawford's a brilliant cook, too.'

'I've heard of him. I didn't know he was her husband. They're quite a famous couple. I suppose I ought to have known, but I'm new in this division.'

'Where are you from then?' Tamara asked. She listened to a life story. She heard what a good job the police service was. She was sympathetic about the difficulties women still faced in it. She agreed that it had its down side. And its up side. And prospects. And problems.

Woman talk. Women's-chores. They rinsed their mugs and turned them upside down to drain.

'I suppose I'd better be getting on,' the constable sighed.

Tamara said. 'Were there signs that anyone else had been in the room? I mean, before—'

'Your own footsteps. You trod in the—'

'I know. I trod in the blood on the floor. But otherwise nothing? I suppose it must be difficult, on that kind of carpet, especially when it was so dirty anyway.'

'You noticed a lot, considering! But the place was a tip, really. I don't know how she could . . . some people!'

'She had been away, and ill.'

'All the same, the dust and fluff of ages. And stains and spills. It didn't look as though anything had been cleaned since they moved in. Fancy sleeping in that. How some people live! You wouldn't believe what I see in this job, honestly, you go into some houses and the state they are in, just everyday life, you know.'

'So not much for the forensics?'

'Of course it isn't for me to say, but I shouldn't think so.'

'Suicide, then.'

'Up to the coroner. I've made a note of Professor Crawford's allegation. But I shouldn't think . . . she lives in another world, doesn't she? A bit of an intellectual.'

Tamara showed the other woman to the front door.

'I saw her on television once, on a quiz show. She wiped the floor with the others. The questionmaster introduced her as the beautiful professor, and she nearly walked out.'

'I saw that too. She told me she won out of fury, it gave her such a buzz,' Tamara said.

'She must have been beautiful though, when she was young.'

Tamara closed the front door, and, on the way to fetch her bags, paused by the gilt-framed mirror in the hall.

That girl can't have been more than six or seven years younger than I am, she thought, but she could only see Thea's beauty in the past tense.

She peered at her own face. Am I a different generation, an older woman, on the shelf; past it? The reflection did not say so. Even when Tamara screwed her features into a smile, only the faintest lines appeared. How long before people say I must have been pretty once?

How long before it's too late? Tick tock, tick . . . the biological-time clock, as journalists on women's pages so aptly and cruelly called it, was marking out the remaining years of youth. Hurry, marry, hurry, marry. Have children before it is too late.

There was a great incentive to believe what Alastair had said; too great?

Chapter 19

'Professor Crawford said there was blood on her hand, sir.'

'So?'

'She said she never touched anything in the room. She said the blood must have come off the stair rail.'

'Bollocks.'

'I know, sir. But she was very insistent about it.'

'Hysteria.'

'Sir.'

'Professor indeed . . . she's the one who's married to that bloke who got off on a manslaughter rap.'

'Balance of the mind—'

'Believe that you'll believe anything. People like that, they think they can do what they want, any time. She's just making trouble.'

'Sir.'

'Did she have anything to show for it? Blood on her dress?'

'Not that she mentioned, sir.'

'What was the point of it anyway?'

'Professor Crawford thought there must have been someone else in the house. Someone who had got blood on his or her hand, and left it on the stair rail on the way down.'

'A killer. She wants us to think it was murder.'

'It seems so, sir.'

'Clearest case of suicide I ever saw. The woman stuffs herself with sedatives and then slashes her wrists.'

'An overdose, sir?'

'Did I say that? No, she took about half a dozen. Enough to give herself a really long night's sleep, knock herself out good and proper.'

'Could someone else have made her take them, sir?'

'You're as bad as those women. They want clues and detection and solving the murder as though we're playing some kids' game.' The chief inspector's voice carried derisive emphasis. 'Clues! They think we're all bumbling bobbies waiting for Peter bloody Wimsey to solve the bloody murder. Were there any clues? Did you see anything I missed then?'

'Nothing out of place that I could see, no, sir.'

'I told you to ask if anyone else had been noticed round the place.'

'None of the neighbours saw anyone. Most of them had gone out for the day and the ones who stayed in were glued to the box, or asleep. Too wet for gardening.'

'Rained all day, didn't it?'

'Yessir. Until five-thirty, according to the weather people.'

'A rainy Sunday in Buriton, enough to cut your throat for even if you hadn't just lost your husband. And the woman had just come out of hospital, right? Depressed, lonely . . . I suppose it's all too simple and human for your professor. These female eggheads . . .'

'She's very good-looking, sir. Well dressed, too.'

'Thought you said she was getting on a bit.'

'Born in 1947.'

'Well then.'

'You wouldn't know it, though. She was wearing a lovely suit, it had little gilt buttons and a sort of braid all round the—'

'When I want an inventory of a witness's wardrobe, I'll tell you.'

'Sir.'

'What did the other one say? She's some sort of bluestocking too, isn't she?'

'Dr Tamara Hoyland. She didn't say much actually, just that she had gone in to check after her friend—'

'I've come across that name somewhere. Hoyland. Is it on the computer?'

'No, sir.'

'Funny that. I could swear I . . . not that it matters. She didn't add anything, did she?'

'Not really. She'd come over from Arthur's Castle, that's up on the north—'

'Arthur's Castle? Why didn't you say so?'

'Sir?'

'Is the woman staying there?'

'I think . . . I mean, yes, sir. She's with her boy fr—'

But the Detective Chief Inspector had already withdrawn his attention from the woman police constable. He dialled a number, and tapped his fingers impatiently while he waited for a reply. 'Come on, come on,' he muttered. 'Oh, there you are. That you? I've got something for you. A witness in a suicide, that's by the way, it's an open-and-shut verdict. But guess where the witness is staying. Arthur's Castle. Yes, that's right. That's what I said. No, of course I don't need any more evidence from her, I told you, it's perfectly straightforward, except for some silly woman trying to muck it up with a fairy story, no need to take any notice of all that, but it gives us a chance to go up there and— what's that? Don't you worry, I'll think of something. Warrant? I wouldn't have thought it was really— yeah, maybe you've got something there. I'll get on to it right away. Arthur's Castle, what a stroke of luck, eh? Thought you'd be pleased.'

Chapter 20

Tamara was just leaving the house when Thea rang from the university to tell her to wait. 'No need to get a taxi. I have to drive up the coast to see some find or other. A couple of German campers turned it up and a council enforcement officer reported it. So I'll give you a lift to Arthur's Castle.'

They drove from the small-scale, wind-sculpted landscape of the far west on to the new trunk road, and then quickly up the spine of Cornwall until they had to turn north to crawl along behind container lorries and, even this early in the year, caravans.

'It's like a foreign country to me, I never come here,' Thea said, hesitating at a crossroads and taking the road that was signposted Tintagel.

'This is a bit of a detour,' Tamara said, and as they crawled in a queue of tourists through Tintagel village, she read out loud the signposts and advertisements for food and souvenirs; all validated, however tenuously, by vaunted association with the local legend. Agravane, Bedivere, Kay, an alphabet of Arthurian knights, their King, Queen, Magician and lost leader. Lancelot patronised biscuits, fudge, models of knights in armour and coarse pottery.

'It's all such nonsense,' the ever-intellectual Thea Crawford moaned. 'Where do they get it all from?'

Tamara had read up the factual basis for the Arthurian legends before coming to Cornwall. She explained to Thea that there was a confusion between two entities, one a literary invention. By analogy, she said, in a few centuries' time people might believe there was a factual basis for the Sherlock Holmes legend. The story-teller, Geoffrey of Monmouth, lived centuries later than the events he purported to describe. He might have worked his imagination on a basis of foggy early folklore; but quite soon other tales that had originally been quite separate were woven together, so that the quest for the Holy Grail, Excalibur or the Sword in the Stone, the Round Table, and Tristan and Isolde eventually seemed to be part of the same saga.

The other basis of the legend was a shadowy figure who might or might not have been a British war leader against the encroaching Anglo-Saxons of the fifth and sixth centuries AD. The conflated story satisfied a romantic and natural need for a hero-king who would come again in times of national trouble.

'But now it just satisfies the demands of the tourist trade,' Tamara said.

'I find it offensive,' Thea said. 'How can people believe such nonsense.'

'It's natural. It's human.'

Once long ago, as a postgraduate student, Tamara had gone to Italy for Easter with the Crawfords. She and Sylvester had tramped the hills of Tuscany together while Thea stayed beside the pool and deepened her suntan. On other days they wandered round the streets and shops of Florence and Siena, checking out the kitchen departments, the clothes being worn by the locals that year, the colour of their bathroom fitments.

'Aren't you at all interested in ordinary people, in modern life?' Tamara had protested, and been amused by Sylvester's giggle.

'You have known Thea long enough to know that she has a restricted range of interests,' he had remarked. But Tamara had been incredulous. 'If you care so passionately about the cooking pots and tools of the distant past, how can you be so indifferent to those of the present day?' And Thea explained that her interest in archaeology was purely for its intellectual challenge and nothing to do with contemporary anthropology or sociology. 'She lives in her own world,' Sylvester said, indulgent while he was mellowed by sun and chianti but sometimes infuriated by his wife's indifference to most of the subjects that concerned him. She managed, politely and elegantly but quite unmistakably, to distance herself from discussion of politics, current affairs, wars and personalities, the currency of a successful journalist's world, and had been known to pick up a book and read it at her own dinner table while her guests argued about a subject that bored her.

Older and wiser now, Tamara made no attempt to discuss the charms of hills and streams, cliff and coast with Thea as they drove through north Cornwall. Instead they spoke of their own subject, the land use and living patterns of prehistoric people in this little-altered landscape. A team of excavators from Thea's department was at work ahead of the bulldozers in a village near Wadebridge, where a new housing estate would create the first residential use of a barren hillside since the Bronze Age. Thea intended to look in on them first. She was late and in a hurry, so Tamara jumped out at the gates to Arthur's Castle and Thea drove straight off.

'Good afternoon,' Tamara said to Ben Oriel. 'Not so wet today.'

'Shall I run you down?' he said.

'No, it's all right, I don't mind walking.' On foot, Tamara could see that the drive was not as perfectly kept as it had seemed from a car two days before. There were tracks where someone had driven off the road and the branches of the shrubs were broken where a vehicle had passed. She turned off into the scrub and walked a little way along the tyre tracks. They led to a tumbledown cottage, its walls covered with ivy, almost swallowed by the encroaching vegetation. Some underclothes and a shirt flapped from a sagging fence. Tamara looked through a broken, dirty window. Somebody lived or camped here. She went on round to an outhouse, almost invisible in the encroaching ivy. Her nose touched a cobweb and she sneezed. There was a rustling noise inside. Tamara, intrepid about nearly all other hazards, was terrified of rats.

She turned briskly away, walking downhill towards the track. At the bridge she paused to scan the water for fish, and standing there on the slab bridge, listened to the unique silence of somewhere that was far from industry and airport. The vegetation suddenly smelt of spring. Tamara picked a handful of violets and primroses and buried her nose in their damp sweetness.

'That's a pretty sight.'

'Hullo, Sir Hubert. I was on my way back to the castle.'

'I'm delighted to see you. We were afraid that you had deserted us.'

'I must apologise for disappearing so unceremoniously yesterday,' Tamara said. 'I was called away rather suddenly.'

They walked together towards the sea. Hubert Blair said, 'England in the spring. It makes one feel quite romantic.'

'Are you a country person?'

'I'm a Shropshire lad. And you're the lass from glorious Devon.'

'You have been checking up on me.'

'We have an acquaintance in common.'

Tamara glanced at the closed, cautious face. 'Who's that?' she said.

'My poetic colleague from the Department of the Environment. There was a verse of his in last week's TLS, did you happen to see it? Quite vivid and evocative, I thought. But perhaps he showed it to you before publication.'

'I haven't seen Mr Black for years,' Tamara said.

'You have taken to describing the past instead of having an influence on the future. Writing a book, I gather.'

'It is called The Early Iron Age in Western Europe.'

They came out on to the stretch of sand. The tide was low, and the little cove, now in the shade of the cliffs, was dank and chilly and suffused by the stench of seaweed. It seemed a beach for shipwrecks in this light, not for happy family holidays, and in a flash of uncharacteristic fantasy Tamara saw the spars of salted driftwood, the frayed lengths of orange rope and the lidless plastic bottles, stained with oil, that are the invariable furniture of any modern tide line, as the remains of unimaginable marine disasters. Shivering, she pulled her coat closely around her throat.

And was it imagination that her companion had let the mask of geniality slip? Glancing back at him as she began to climb the rock steps, Tamara saw the face of a ruthless and greedy man, calculating profits.

He said suddenly, 'It won't do. You know that.'

'What won't do?' Tamara asked.

'Your young man. He'll have to come clean about his discoveries.'

'I don't know what you mean.'

'You should persuade him of it. You know what's what. Get him to tell his tale and be done. Place, map references, all the details he brought back. You must have your own methods of persuasion – lucky chap that he is, young Dr Hope.'

Unable to think of anything to say, Tamara said nothing. Sir Hubert Blair went on, panting slightly, but still hauling himself up the steep slope at her heels. 'What a lot of trouble we should save if you spill the beans yourself. It's valuable information, as of course you are aware. The Foundation is not ungenerous.'

'Are you suggesting that I should sell you Alastair's secrets, Sir Hubert?'

'A small token of appreciation might change hands. Get yourself a trousseau, perhaps. Or regard it as a wedding present.'

'Sir Hubert, even if I—'

'I've heard a good deal about you, what with one thing and another. To quote the good doctor, you have a bottom of good sense.'

'I disagree with most of Dr Johnson's aphorisms, as it happens,' Tamara said.

'That's as may be, but you know that Hope can't keep it all secret, whatever his motives for wanting to. He's a dear chap, your young man, heart of gold, high principles, well meaning, but not what you would call practical. But when we think of your good self, with your experience of the real world . . .'

'What exactly did you want me to tell you?' Tamara said. She stood waiting as her companion joined her on the windy plateau. Daylight was almost gone; the lamps on either side of the castle door beckoned to late-comers, flares of multi-coloured light.

'Just give me the details of what he found and where. No need to let on to the dear fellow, let him go on thinking he's kept everything to himself, we can save so much argument and soul-searching. Quite improper, of course, his results are the Foundation's property, but I'm not sure that the Grail Foundation should have them either. This is becoming a matter of the national interest, as I told Tom Black this morning. He assured me that you could be relied on in such circumstances.'

This man thinks I am a fool, Tamara thought. She said, 'I

really don't know anything about it. But presumably you have explained all this to Alastair himself today.'

'Miss Hoyland.' Major Griggs came tripping towards her, hand outstretched. 'What a pleasant surprise.'

'Alastair said he'd tell you I was coming back.'

'You must come inside and get warm. Let me take your coat. Come you in, I'll hang it here, and then . . . but were you expecting Dr Hope to get here ahead of you? Hasn't he come with you?'

'He came over this morning, quite early.'

'Perhaps he had some other calls to make on the way. He isn't here.'

It was by then late afternoon, and Alastair had left Buriton hours before. 'He was going to come straight to Arthur's Castle,' Tamara said. 'He seemed to think there was some urgency when you rang.'

'I didn't speak to him,' Major Griggs said.

'Wasn't it you? I thought he said so.'

'I am afraid he took a very final farewell yesterday,' Sir Hubert Blair said reproachfully. 'Our discussions were not what you would call fruitful. I won't deny that we were disappointed.'

'I'm sorry, I don't quite . . .'

Count Kowalski came out of the solar and stood looming over Tamara. He smelt of some slightly herbal scent, but there was a tiny spot of grease on his tie. Tall and still physically powerful, he seemed, for a moment, genuinely menacing. Tamara looked round the bright, warm hall, and then she shivered and said.

'No, I won't take my coat off, I really mustn't stay on my own. I expect Alastair has been held up, I ought to be getting back to London.'

She turned towards the door. Major Griggs and Sir Hubert were standing with their backs to it and neither moved.

'Don't go yet,' the Major said.

'We'd like a chance to talk to you,' the Count said.

'Won't you stay the night? Your room is waiting for you,' the Major said.

'Thanks so much, I think I should order a cab and catch the last train.'

Without looking at his watch, the Count said, 'I think you

are too late for it now.' He put out his left hand and snapped the lights on. The artificial flare, on the wall beside him, brought the fierce angles of his face into sudden prominence. Tamara looked at the three men. She tilted her head, swept her eyelids slowly down and up.

'Well, perhaps after all I should accept your kind—', she began, when on the other side of the hall the lift doors were heard to open. Along with the three men, she turned to see one of the security guards come into the hall, followed by two men in plain clothes and the woman police constable Tamara had spoken to that morning.

'They didn't let me ring through,' the fat boy said immediately. 'Honest, sir, I did try.'

'That's all right, Macintosh,' Major Griggs said. He marched to meet the new arrivals. One of them offered his identity card.

'Devon and Cornwall Constabulary, sir, making enquiries into the death of Dr Louise Dench.'

'Dr – ? Oh, the lady who was here yesterday, how tragic, I had no idea. But I don't think we can help you, officer, I don't believe any of us saw her, except for one of Macintosh's colleagues, one of our security men.'

'I saw her here,' Tamara said clearly. She edged past the Count to go towards the police party. 'Hullo again, Constable Parkin, I told you all about it didn't I? Would you like me to go through it again?'

The older, larger of the two men replied. 'You'll be Dr Hoyland. No, that won't be necessary, thank you. I've got your evidence here, unless you have anything to add to it.'

'No, I think I said everything I could this morning, but if you don't need me now, would it be all right if I carried on? I was just going to ring for a cab, I want to get back to London tonight.'

He looked at his watch. 'You'll be a bit pushed to catch the last train. Why don't you run her down to Bodmin, Sheila? That's it, Miss Hoyland, Constable Parkin will give you a lift and come back here for us afterwards. Go on, Sheila, you know what to do.'

For a second day running Tamara left Arthur's Castle with a sensation of escaping. 'This is very kind of you,' she said automatically as the shining car swept past the empty guard hut.

'Think nothing of it, you'd do the same for me.'

Tamara glanced at her, a little surprised, and the other girl went on, 'You could have said who you were this morning.'

'What do you mean?'

'It just came through on the computer before we were leaving, your rating, I mean.'

'My rating.'

'AEF. Afford Every Facility. My boss thought he knew your name even before that, he's got a mind like a computer himself.'

Then he must be several years behind the times too, Tamara thought but did not say. 'I'm very grateful. This is a great help.'

'I know I'm not allowed to ask any questions.'

'I have got one though. Was there a packet of photographs in Louise Dench's house, in her pocket maybe? Pictures of some old-looking buildings, jungle, tribesmen standing beside them, just a stack of prints with an elastic band round them.'

'Nothing like that. There were some albums with wedding photos, that was all.'

'Oh, I just wondered, something we talked about when we met before.' Tamara leant back and closed her eyes over their miserable prickling.

'Want some music?' Sheila Parkin twiddled to the local radio station. 'Easy listening,' she said.

Tamara's thoughts moved round a circular track and repeatedly brought her back to the same starting line. She had made a mistake, and made it again. Last night Alastair had disarmed her. He had persuaded her of his innocence. She had believed him. She never doubted, when he set off from Buriton this morning, that he was coming to Arthur's Castle.

He wound me round his finger, she thought.

The disc jockey chose an uncharacteristically classical piece, an aria from the Marriage of Figaro.

How did he convince me so easily? Where is my training and experience, what is wrong with me, that I am such a bad picker of men? First Kim, now Alastair . . .

Tamara closed her eyes. '*Se vuol' ballare, signore contino* . . .' The voice was mellow, persuasive; like Alastair Hope's. If you want to dance, you'll dance to my tune.

Chapter 21

The visit to the building site near Wadebridge took Thea much longer than intended and it was dusk before she got to the camp site where a Celtic head had turned up. The campers, who had squatted on the cliff top site relatively recently, were obviously the target of local venom, and the man who reported the find clearly hoped that it would prove to be stolen.

Thea went in with the distaste she felt for the aspirations of those people, so many of them her own students, who chose 'the simple life'. Among her kinder epithets were 'woolly thinking' and 'semi-educated dupes'.

Thea assumed that they supposed themselves to be recreating a golden age by rejecting the late twentieth century. Existence without the benefits of civilisation was squalid and always had been, even in those distant periods that were her field of study. The world was naturally dirty and dangerous; when uncontrolled by artificial means, it was red in tooth, claw and weapon, and the lives of the primitive peoples Thea studied had been nasty, brutish and short. She had neither sympathy for sentimental notions about noble savages nor comprehension of spiritual yearnings for unscientific superstition.

Thea glanced unenthusiastically around, aware that her attitude must seem offensively disdainful to the people who, openly or otherwise, were watching her. An overweight middle-aged man came to show her the way across the littered ground. Candles and battery lamps were being lit in the draughty shelters and the wailing of children and barking of dogs competed with several varieties of music, all with powerful thudding beats. A long-haired man was playing tunes from the nineteen sixties on a guitar. Reggae was blaring from the radio of a large blue car, most of which was shrouded under a billowing tarpaulin.

Treading delicately in her suede boots, Thea crossed the field to the wall that separated it from the coastal footpath and the edge of the cliff. The granite head had been found nearby, as though the stone had been re-used to build the wall, and that was how one would expect to come upon an ancient artefact. But this one was not ancient. It had been carved with a metal chisel and had no likeness to any supposedly contemporary Celtic object. It was a pastiche.

A wasted afternoon. Hugging her cashmere coat tightly around her, Thea picked her way back to her car.

The most objectionable aspect of this dump, she thought, was that while proclaiming their devotion to simplicity, its residents all possessed so many, such expensive consumer goods. Where did they get the money for saxophones and sound systems, for waterproof tents and large motor cars? Thea ducked under a damp towel pegged to a tent rope. How could they afford such good quality equipment? Pinched from their wretched parents, no doubt, she concluded, noticing a tattered young woman carrying a bulging green and tan leather suitcase with an expensive brand label into her tent.

They were scavengers and spongers, and Thea, who supposed herself to be entirely apolitical, drove away in a self-righteously right-wing rage.

Pain.

Darkness.

Pain, darkness, cold.

His eyes were covered. He could not move. He could not see.

Where? What?

Alastair Hope had woken and relapsed into oblivion several times before he achieved even fitful awareness.

A sound. Footsteps. Tamara.

He drifted in and out of consciousness.

He was lying on his side, his shoulder and hip bone pressed

on to an unyielding surface. Ankles and wrists were tied together and tethered. Over his face and pulled tight round the neck was a cloth. When he opened his eyes he saw nothing but blackness. There was a gag in his mouth. He had thrown up. He had evacuated bowel and bladder where he lay.

He had never known such thirst. He had never known such pain.

After a while he thought, come, let's be thankful for small mercies. Any medical man would expect me to inhale and suffocate on my own vomit.

At least he was still alive.

Just.

Tamara's journey was rendered hideous by the rival cacophonies from inadequately shielded headphones attached to personal stereos, and when she moved into another carriage, it was only to find it full of beer-drinking hymn-singers, with large labels on their suitcases showing them to be members of a group called the Praisemakers. They were on the first leg of a long journey to the west coast of the United States, and alternated their repetition of banal sentiments with roars of 'California, here we come'.

In a way the distraction from her own preoccupation was no bad thing. Would Alastair be back in the flat, or wouldn't he? Will he, won't he, praise him, praise him . . .

He was not. The place was as orderly as Tamara's Portuguese cleaner always left it. The plants climbed healthily towards the skylight, the pretty yew and cherrywood furniture shone, the paisley cushions were plumped, the wood fire laid ready for a match in the delft-tiled fireplace of what had once been the top-floor nursery in the Kensington mansion.

Alastair had not been back. The few belongings that he, always a light traveller, had brought over with him when he moved in were still neatly disposed in the cupboard. When Tamara opened the door she winced at the familiar smell. She caught sight of her own reflection in the mirror.

Nobody from Department E would recognise me, she thought.

Where is the self-controlled, composed, assured operator that the active secret agent used to be? For that matter, where was the intellectual, the professional woman?

The distraught image of someone blown off course by emotion and unreason had nothing to do with the person Tamara believed herself to be.

She lifted the receiver in a slightly trembling hand and rang Cornwall's general hospital in Truro. Nobody of Alastair's description had been brought in. This was where any casualty in the county would have come, unless Plymouth was nearer. She rang Plymouth. He was not known there either. She rang the police. He had not been involved in any reported accident.

She tried Alastair's sister. Had he turned up there, returning perhaps to the flat that had been his London base before he met Tamara? 'He hasn't been here for days,' the lightly Scottish voice said. 'Anyway, two of my son's friends are living in the basement now, he'll have to find himself somewhere else now.'

A call to her own parents. Tamara would have to postpone her visit but she would see them soon. Everything all right, down in Devon? Her mother made no mention of Alastair. She would have mentioned it if he had come there.

Tamara rang Thea Crawford. Had she left her diary? 'Are you on your own?' Tamara prompted, unable to bring herself to ask the question directly. 'When will Sylvester be back?' No word of Alastair. He had not gone back there either.

He had scarpered. It was necessary to accept it. He had disappeared.

In the small hours the tenant of the second-floor flat came upstairs to complain of the footsteps above her head. 'I wouldn't say anything, but I was up all last night too. I really need the sleep.'

'I'm sorry. I'll stop,' Tamara said. She had hardly been aware of restlessly, regularly, pacing up and down.

The woman, a gynaecologist, paused before going back to bed. 'Are you all right? Do you need help?'

'No thanks very much. I'm fine.'

Help, perhaps. But not from a physician.

From the police? Or the reverse; should she tell the police in Buriton what she now believed to be the case? It was probably her duty to say that Alastair was – no, that was too unequivocal; that he could be, might be involved in the death of Louise Waugh. That, suspected by Tamara, he had run away.

For the remaining hours of the night Tamara lay rigidly flat in the large bed, not trespassing on to what already seemed to be Alastair's side. She forced herself to keep still, to keep her eyes closed.

At dawn she reached a decision. She would go to Department E, crawl back, tail between legs, to the obscure office where Thomas Black, CBE, ostensibly eked out the dull days of an unglamorous civil servant, and get his advice. He, perhaps alone in the world, knew all there was to know about Tamara. It had often been a source of irritation to her that the information he had derived from positive vetting, from public knowledge and from his own informed judgement should be so complete. 'He knows more about me than I do myself,' she had once complained to his secretary, Mrs Uglow. 'It's his stock in trade,' Mrs Uglow replied. 'But don't worry about it. Nothing shocks him.'

It would not be the first time that Mr Black had seen Tamara deceived by a man.

She dressed carefully in the morning and put on more cosmetics than usual, to show a brave shop-front, but her steps faltered as she drew near Whitehall.

What could Mr Black actually do, if Alastair had fled the country? The chances of any passport officer having noticed him were minuscule. Within the United Kingdom a citizen could still drop out without trace. Mr Black was not a Father Confessor, and Tamara did not need absolution. Forgiveness for credulity, perhaps, and from whom better than the man who had trained her in cynicism; but the desire to unload her troubles was puerile.

In St James's Park, near the very bridge over the very water where drama's heroes and villains so often discuss duplicity on television, Tamara sat on the green bench on which story-tellers' imaginary spies and spy masters traditionally plan their dirty deeds. No experienced viewer could ever suppose that the view or the passers-by were exactly what they seemed.

Was Alastair's disappearance what it seemed?

A man who looked more like a secret agent than Tamara ever could, sat down at the other end of the bench.

Could there be another explanation for Alastair's absence? She had jumped to a conclusion. Had he really committed an iniquity, been detected and made his escape?

The man laid his tweed hat on the seat beside him and unbuttoned his jacket. He began to struggle with a cellophane packet of sandwiches.

Was there an alternative explanation for what had happened?

The man put away the bunch of keys with which he had tried to puncture the sandwich wrapping and used a lighted match to burn a hole in it. He grinned at Tamara. 'If there's a better way, you tell me,' he said.

A better way.

Was there a better way for a man's girlfriend to react to unexplained behaviour than to assume that he was a criminal? What made her so sure that he had chosen to disappear? He could have driven off from Buriton the previous morning and been held up on his way to Arthur's Castle.

The sandwiches were sardine. They smelt disgusting.

But there had not been an accident. The police and hospitals had not heard of him.

Had he simply changed his mind and changed his plans?

But then he would have let Tamara know. If, that is, he could get to a telephone.

'You're miles away, aren't you?' The sandwich-eater brushed crumbs from his protuberant stomach.

'Sorry, what?'

'A penny for them.'

Tamara stared without seeing him. What Alastair knew was worth much more than pennies. The exact location of a lost city, El Dorado or not, was valuable information.

'Can't be chained to a word processor for the rest of the day without some sustenance.'

Was Alastair chained somewhere, confined, imprisoned?

'Tammy.' The man slid closer to Tamara, and waved his hand to and fro before her blank and absent gaze.

'Wake up, Tam, we've got some talking to do.' He crumpled the litter and lobbed it past her into the wire basket.

'Who are you?'

'Don't you remember me? Carl Hawker, *The Argus*. The last time was a few years ago on Forway.'

'Nobody calls me Tam. Or Tammy.'

'And I saw you in Cornwall.'

'Have you been following me?'

'I have been wondering what you're up to.'

'Were you in Buriton on Sunday?' Tamara said, recalling a faintly familiar figure in the university park.

'That's it. You didn't recognise me.'

Tamara twitched at her wandering attention like a driver putting a car into gear. She looked at Carl Hawker. He was about the same age as herself, tough and knowing. A print journalist; his appearance was not, presumably, televisual. He was overweight, with small eyes, thin, crooked lips and acne scars.

He said, 'You were at Arthur's Castle.'

'Are you doing a story about it?'

'I am now. When I see Hubert Blair, Kowalski and one of Tom Black's young Turks in the same place . . .'

Carl Hawker had been covering a story on the island of Forway when Tamara was sent there by Department E. Of course he was in a position to find out that she was more than the innocent fieldworking archaeologist everyone else had taken her to be. She supposed she should be grateful to him for not writing anything about her then.

'I left Department E some time ago,' she said. 'I just went to Arthur's Castle to keep my boyfriend company. I wouldn't have thought there was much for you there.'

'Wouldn't you?'

A flight of ducks rose in unison from the water and headed west. 'I've got to get back to Cornwall today,' Tamara said, the decision to return coming at the same time as the words. 'But we could have lunch together. There's a restaurant—'

'I know. It can be on *The Argus*.'

They walked side by side. Carl Hawker's eyes watched all the passers-by. He doesn't miss a thing, Tamara thought. They spoke of the book she was writing.

'I am going to do a book soon,' Carl said. 'Write something

that doesn't end up as the fish and chip wrapping.' But it was not until they were sitting down in a restaurant much patronised by politicians that he told her what he was working on at the moment. 'You can say what you like here. They are all so interested in themselves that nobody listens to anyone else.'

The personality involved was Hector Kowalski; the story was to do with his financial dealings. Tamara did not understand a word of it.

Carl stopped talking and looked at her. 'This is double-Dutch to you.'

'I don't understand the language.'

'Oh God, not another one who always skips the city pages.'

'Another one?'

'Maggie. My wife.'

'A photographer? She was on Forway that time too.'

'That's right. That was before we got married. We've got two kids now, she's got some excuse for not understanding economics. But you, Tammy – Tamara – you ought to know about money, real money, high finance, if you meddle in politics the way you do. Oh, come on, Tamara, don't pretend with me.'

'OK. And you've got a point, maybe I should have taken some interest, but I don't need to any more. I told you, I am just an archaeologist now.'

'So why were you following Kowalski on Sunday?'

'I wasn't. I saw him in Buriton by coincidence. I have no idea what he was doing there, but I was staying with Thea Crawford.'

'Sylvester's wife?'

'Anyway, what were you doing there yourself? Were you following me?'

'I was nosing around.'

'And I suppose you know what the Count was up to?'

'He was chatting up the students. He asked where a couple of the dons lived.'

'I wonder why.'

'Dench and Yule, they were called. And then, as you won't be surprised to hear, he went off arm-in-arm to his fancy car with one of the girls. God knows how he manages it at his age.'

Carl Hawker made appreciative noises about his *magret de*

canard. Tamara picked at her salad without interest. She said,

'I don't understand why you were there in the first place. You can't really have been following me.'

'Not really, though seeing you certainly made the story more interesting. No, it's a piece for the colour supplement about money pirates. The buccaneers of our time, men like Kowalski who make their killings on the money market. He's a good example because he's always had style. Sees what he wants, takes it and comes out smelling of roses.'

'What's his secret?'

'Instant action. No dithering, no delegation. Sees what he wants and goes out to get it, as simple as that. But what I don't know is what's in it for him with the Grail Foundation.'

Tamara thought, I know what's in it for him. I must go back. She glanced up at Carl Hawker's avid, shrewd face. He was watching her like a predatory animal. Tamara opened her eyes wide and stretched her mouth into merriment. She began to eat with apparent appreciation, and to listen to a knowledgeable run-down of modern financial dodges with every appearance of enthralment, of admiration. Carl Hawker was clever; but better men than he had succumbed to those experienced wiles and he had given more than he gained by the time that, a trifle unsteadily, he handed a perfectly sober Tamara into her taxi.

Later.

Hours, days later?

He tested what he could. It was hard to distinguish the agonies of cramp from those caused by injury. He could flex the muscles in his limbs, though weakly. He did not think they were broken. It hurt to breathe. Throat and larynx sore. He could move his head a tiny distance but doing so sent a lancing pain through the skull, as did rolling the eyes.

He diagnosed an infection of the upper respiratory tract and a head wound.

Afraid.

Cold. Thirsty. In pain.

Wounded, bound, abandoned.

How long? Where?

He could hear nothing, see nothing, smell nothing but his own ordure.

I might die here, Alastair Hope thought.

Here. Where?

Where am I?

Why?

Chapter 22

The car would have been left to break up where it fell, at the bottom of three-hundred-foot cliffs, if the officers of the Air Sea Rescue Service had been perfectly certain that nobody was in or under it.

'Couldn't have survived, not a fall like that,' the reporter from the *Cornish Times* said.

A couple of agency photographers were craning perilously over the sheer drop.

'Quite an overhang down there.'

'That's why they have to get the whole thing up.'

'Because of the overhang?'

'It isn't safe for the divers.'

Someone was dangling below the helicopter. A figure clothed in fluorescent orange waterproofs swung gymnastically on to the car's body. After a while, he began to attach hawsers under the roof.

'When did it go over, anyway?' said a photographer.

'It must have been last night.'

'You couldn't see it at high tide.'

'That's a good shot.' The video man aimed his camera eagerly. The helicopter pilot had brought his craft too close to the cliffs. Pulling away, he dragged the rescuer off his perch to sway, momentarily out of control, above the surging waves.

'It's not worth the effort,' a woman said. She held tightly on to the leashes of her pair of spaniels, and kept carefully to the coastal footpath. 'Not just to recover a body.'

'They like the challenge,' her companion said. 'It's very boring to be a peace-time serviceman, no fun if there's no action. You need an enemy.' He swished his blackthorn cane against the gaudy gorse without felling any.

By midday there had been occasional gleams of sunshine although the wind had hardly dropped and everyone was still muffled in hoods and hats, but there were enough watchers by this time to line the cliff top like a rank of soldiers.

A young woman who was walking along the coast path nodded at an acquaintance, before saying, 'How morbid,' and continuing briskly on her way.

'I like watching experts at work,' he called after her, but soon he moved away himself, and when the battered hunk of metal was finally landed, the afternoon light was already fading and the audience had dwindled to a few children and idlers, to make a background for the indefatigable photographers and reporters. One of them peered at the remnants of the number plate, scribbling the figures in his notebook.

'Move back there, please,' a policeman insisted. 'Stand well clear.'

'Will there be fingerprints?' a boy demanded, and was answered by the sight of a plain-clothes official pulling plastic gloves on before trying to open the boot.

Tamara would retrace Alastair's movements and hope that something might turn up.

On the way she tried to think herself into the detachment that was the most valuable asset of both academic and agent. Somewhere during the last few weeks she had lost the lifelong habit of dispassion. She would treat the search as just another assignment; not so much a quest, in the Grail Foundation's terminology, as a commission for which she was well qualified.

It was a relief to be in her own car, elderly by now, since she had bought cheaply the specially modified machine provided by Department E. Some of its refinements had been removed. She no longer had, for example, a telephone. But it was still in disguise, as unrecognisable for what it was as a tank that looked like a tractor.

Going to Cornwall as Alastair's appendage had been curiously lowering to the spirits although Tamara had not defined it at the time. Now she was in control.

Buzzing along the motorway at a higher than legal speed, she played the Mozart opera of which she had heard snatches the day before. She thought, somebody is going to dance to my tune now. When the last chorus ended and the tape popped out of its slot, she found herself listening to the radio news. Its last item was about a car that had gone over the cliffs in north Cornwall. Naval divers had concluded that it was empty at the time, and it had been winched up to land. The car was a dark blue Volvo.

A blue Volvo.

At first Tamara did not take the information in, then it registered on her brain. A Volvo. Dark blue.

It was a sporty-looking car, very solid and fast, far too expensive but irresistible, said Alastair, who had gone out with the intention of buying a third- or fourth-hand family saloon. As passenger, Tamara had felt a little queasy as it swung round the bends. But the driver had a great time; and when Tamara took her turn at the wheel she understood the temptation to which Alastair had succumbed.

How was anyone sure it had been empty?

How was she sure that it was Alastair's car?

Tamara pulled in at the next motorway service station, for the first time in two years regretting that she no longer had her own car telephone, and managed, after several calls to the wrong police station or to the wrong person at the right place, to get through to someone who both knew and would divulge the number of the car. Its battered shell had by this time been stored in a secure, official place. The car was easily identifiable.

The still decipherable numbers etched on the engine parts and windows had been compared with a central register. And, of course, the number had been run through the central computer.

It was Alastair's car.

'Are you certain it was empty? That nobody was driving when it went over? How can you be sure?'

But Tamara knew how they could be sure, and shook herself away from hysteria. The gear must have been in neutral, the handbrake off, the windows closed, the doors locked. That car had been pushed over the cliff. If it had not been high tide it would have burst into flames. As it was, there might be identifiable fingerprints on the coachwork.

A man who needed to go into hiding because he had been detected as a murderer might well have made such a plan; and might have ditched the car in such a way that its driver was supposed drowned.

But so could someone else produce the same effect. This was the time to think and act; no more jumping to conclusions, Tamara told herself. She, like the Devon and Cornwall Constabulary, would now search for traces of Alastair Hope.

She would work backwards. The car had been found not far from Arthur's Castle. She had no proof that he had not arrived there the previous day. That was the place to start.

The police checks at Arthur's Castle had disappointed the Superintendent.

'Nothing for us there at all,' his inspector reported. 'The old man lives there most of the year and the others come down for meetings the odd weekend. They have spent a packet on it though, I've never seen anything like it. The materials, the labour . . . it's more like something in Texas or California once you get inside. But nothing suspicious that I could see.'

'Then why are they so determined to keep people away? There must be something going on.'

The young inspector was a graduate of Leeds University who had gone into the police on an accelerated promotion scheme. He believed in using evidence rather than instinct. After the identification of Alastair Hope's car, the vehicle of a recent guest at Arthur's Castle, of the man who was attached to one of the people who found the body, he was annoyed at having to agree that there must be cause for suspicion and investigation at a place whose residents had seemed perfectly irrelevant to him.

His Superintendent was annoyed that there seemed, after all, to be reason to treat Louise Waugh's death as murder. All the details had to be reconsidered with far greater attention and urgency. Professor Crawford had been right. There was a trace of the victim's blood on the banister rail. None was found on the stair carpet or elsewhere in the house, except for a tiny smear on a silk scarf that was screwed up and had been left on the table in the downstairs room.

The scarf had been expensive; made in Italy, with hand rolled edges and an up-market brand name. Further forensic examination showed that it had been in contact with water, French perfume and pipe tobacco.

'How's this for a hypothesis,' the Detective Inspector said. 'He gets invited in for coffee and slips her a mug full of knock-out drops. Then he gets her on to the bed and slashes her wrists with her own kitchen knife.'

'One cut each?' asked the Superintendent.

'No, there were fainter marks too, that's what made us think she'd done it herself. But then a doctor would have known about that too.' It was well established that suicides nearly always cut too lightly at first. A single slash would have been almost incontrovertible evidence of murder.

'It's a chancy murder method.'

'The suspect could well have known that she was taking the blood-thinning medication.'

'He wears gloves and takes care not to step in the blood, but he absent-mindedly touches the stair rail on the way down. Perhaps he's pulling the gloves off as he goes. Anyway, he wipes them, or his hand or something on the scarf and makes his getaway.'

'It was her own scarf, was it?'

'Constable Parkin thinks it was too good for her.'

'That right, Sheila?'

'Well, sir, the deceased's clothes were cheap and nasty, frankly. That was the wardrobe of someone who just wasn't interested. But what she did buy was all in browns and greens, the odd yellow shirt, as though she had been told those were the colours for redheads and never thought about it again. But the scarf is a sort of coral colour, it wouldn't have suited her at all and it was a completely different quality too.'

'Could have been a present from her husband. He might not have been sure what colour she'd have liked,' said the Superintendent, who had considerable experience of the Christmas presents he chose for his wife being exchanged the day after Boxing Day.

'Yes, sir, of course it could, I said that to the Chief Inspector.

Only it was the last colour anyone would have chosen to go with that hair.'

'I suppose this is why we let women into the force.'

'What else have we got? Who saw her last?'

'Tamara Hoyland.'

'We can hardly suspect her,' said the senior officer.

'Ben Oriel's story tallies. He had driven Louise Dench from Arthur's Castle to Buriton and dropped her at the front door. He had not observed any signs of distress or suicidal intention, but did not know her well and would probably not have noticed anyway. Nobody had admitted to seeing her after that.'

'What about the neighbours?'

'Didn't see a thing. It was pouring with rain all day, the ones who hadn't gone out for Sunday drives with the family got their heads down for a zizz.'

'So anyone could have simply knocked at the door and been let in.'

'That's about the size of it. The neighbours on one side are away, on the other they had gone out to lunch with the grandparents, one lot across the road were at the bowling club, another always spend Sundays at the Pentecostal Chapel. You could have murdered a dozen people in the Gloweth estate that day without anyone noticing.'

He was in the private hut.

He had never been allowed inside the private hut.

This is what all the men suffer. I am one of them now. I am their Old Man returned to them. I have come to them in their hour of need.

I am not the Old Man, I am Alastair Hope.

I am delirious. I have a fever.

I am not in the jungle, I am in Britain.

The journey is over.

The women were dancing outside the palisade. They chanted and wailed. Their voices sounded like the wind, like a Scottish wind at home on the moors, howling around the house on a winter night, with the thunder of the sea beyond the fields.

It is the wind. I do not hear the voices of the women. I am not with the People.

Alastair is the Old Man. Alastair will stay with the People for ever. Now he is one of the People.

Pain. Thirst.
Darkness. Cold.

Chapter 23

Count Kowalski and Sir Hubert Blair had every intention of distracting Merlin from the results of the Hope Expedition but they were dismayed to hear him say, before they began their subtle arguments, that he had already changed his mind.

'I am coming round to seeing things in a new way,' he began.

'What are you talking about, exactly?' Sir Hubert asked.

'So I have come to the conclusion that the Foundation should simply write off its investment in the Hope Expedition.'

Lord Collin nodded sagely, as he always did in his increasingly frequent moments of incomprehension. Hubert Blair and Count Kowalski spoke simultaneously.

'We can't do that!'

'That's going too far!'

In a more measured tone, the former civil servant said, 'Perhaps the Chairman would care to expand a little.'

'Who's been getting at him?' Kowalski demanded of Major Griggs. 'Who has he been talking to?'

'He's called Justinian,' Merlin Lloyd began.

'Nobody's called Justinian,' Kowalski growled.

'Except emperors,' Sir Hubert Blair murmured with the self-satisfied chuckle of a man who knew himself to be the only classical scholar in the house.

'He lives a little way along the coast and came to see me yesterday evening,' Merlin went on.

Justinian had been brought along by Ben Oriel, who had spoken of him in a way that caught Merlin's interest.

Ben had sneaked him into the castle through the tunnel and then up in the lift to Merlin's private apartment quite late at night, after the Knights were in bed and Major Griggs off duty.

There was no need to mention it to Major Griggs, Merlin had remarked in a throw-away manner.

Justinian had a smooth, pale brown face, hardly lined, with very clear, very blue eyes and long, straight hair, prematurely – if that face was an indication of age – white. He was stout but not flabby and stood with a kind of unostentatious self-confidence, a man at home in his skin. His clothes, jeans and a knitted sweater, were clean, but crumpled and torn. He looks like an innocent, Merlin thought, and held out his hand. The other man stepped forward to shake it. His touch was, literally, shocking: a warm thrill ran through Merlin's palm, and up his arm, and on through the sentient part of his body into, Merlin would have sworn, the lower limbs that had felt nothing for forty years.

The visitor gazed at him with a kind of gentle, disinterested candour. Without speaking, he deliberately put his hands, side by side, on Merlin's forehead. After pressing for a moment, he moved them to his shoulders and then to his chest. Warmth flowed from his flesh.

Then he stepped back, with a slight, absent-minded smile. 'Enough,' he said.

Merlin, who had been caught in a trance of pleasure, jerked himself into awareness. 'Are you a healer?'

'Some people think so.' His voice was light and musical with a slight New England accent.

'Ben here tells me that you have special faculties and knowledge.'

'I only know what is obvious to anyone with open eyes and mind.'

Merlin leant forward, avid with curiosity. 'Do you know that King Arthur was here?'

'What do you think yourself?'

'No, you tell me.'

'I know it.'

The soft, agreeable voice spoke on and Merlin listened, at first more dispassionately and then in an ecstasy of conviction. Justinian had the answers and the explanations. He made everything fall into place.

Beneath the earth is a hidden, pulsating power, known to stone-age man, who erected temples and monuments at its surge points. The Circles of Silence such as Stonehenge and the Rollright Stones, the less famous and smaller versions in the Celtic west, were the survivors of many that had been destroyed by men too obtuse to understand what they were doing. The nature of the current is forceful, subtle and impossible to define in terms of the dimensions apparent to the senses of modern man. Only those who had studied long and meditated deeply could become initiates into the ancient powers.

'But is it only at stone circles?' Merlin asked.

'Obviously not. You know as well as I do that we are over a place of power here and now. Why else should the ancient kings have built their palace here?'

'I wish I could be sure,' Merlin said.

'Justinian is sure,' Ben Oriel said.

'Ben has touching faith in me,' Justinian said, dropping his arm around the young man's shoulders. 'But human enlightenment has only one instrument. It is an educated mind illuminated by revelation. I have studied and pondered, meditated and, eventually, after many years, I have seen.'

'My own training was as a scientist.'

'But you don't arrogate to yourself the role of substitute for a priest, as so many scientists do. You don't imagine that nobody else is qualified to validate the truth. Your mind is open to believing things that cannot be demonstrated; otherwise, what are you doing here at Arthur's Castle, on the very line of power itself?'

'Are you saying that I could have been brought here by a power I wasn't aware of at the time?' Merlin asked.

'It is only in materialistic western society that the knowledge you have is defined as fantasy. Elsewhere it is common for men to see such forces as clearly as they see the trees and birds; as clearly as I see them.'

'And do similar forces exist all over the world?' Merlin asked.

'Oh, far more so in some places,' Justinian replied immediately. 'Here they are faint and shadowy. But the world still has areas that have escaped corruption. There are still societies in which every man, woman and child has the knowledge and wisdom of the ancients.'

'Where? Could I send a Quest for them?'

'Discovery is destruction unless the explorer is wise. You are in danger of doing a disservice to our planet, Merlin,' Justinian said in a voice of prophetic doom. He was impressive and credible, and he put into words the niggling anxiety that Merlin had already begun to feel.

'You mean the Hope Expedition,' Merlin said.

'The artificial glare of the modern world will wither the lost lore. It will do harm to those who have nurtured it through the millenia,' Justinian said sternly.

'Don't we need the lost wisdom of the ancients?'

Justinian, who had been standing straight but relaxed in front of Merlin's chair and gazing down on him, withdrew his mesmeric stare and moved across to the great wall of glass.

'I can understand your motives,' he said kindly. 'I'm sure you weren't interested in simple profit. But you need to think it through. Here at Arthur's Castle you are trying to revive the cult of the Once and Future King, of Logres and the Matter of Britain, because you mourn its loss. But ask yourself how it died. What destroyed it?' He looked like a preacher. A century earlier he would have made a remarkable religious reformer, inspired by his own conviction. The long fingers of his right hand moved from side to side in emphasis, the light winking regularly on a great green ring.

'It's all connected. You can't separate Arthur from the lines of energy, or what happened here so long ago from what is happening now in Africa, in Indonesia, in New Guinea, in the Amazon, in all the places where nature has held out against the modern world. We know what the mocking materialists say. They claim that there was no chivalry. They say King Arthur and his knights were brutal, squalid aggressors. They tell us that life in the middle ages was short and cruel. They try to persuade us that the simple peoples of the earth live in poverty and pain. They tell us we are romantic, or sentimental, deluded by our own dreams.'

'The number of times I have heard that,' Merlin murmured.

'Arthur was defeated by the barbarian hordes, and now other barbarians are poised to defeat other Arthurs: and are you, Merlin, the namesake, are you going to take your share in destroying another kingdom?'

The next morning, in the cold light of a grey day, Merlin realised that he had been to some degree hypnotised. He was a good subject, and had undergone the experience during his quests for a cure. He did not mind; what Justinian said was no less true when considered coldly and dispassionately.

All the same, I went a bit overboard for that bloke, he thought. How had he known all about the Hope Expedition?

Never mind. It did not matter how he knew, he was certainly sincere. That had not been an act. And there was good sense in what he said. As a one-time scientist, Merlin could agree the need for some representatives of primitive man to remain upon the earth. It was no different from protecting and conserving threatened species of plants or animals. There was no knowing when one apparently insignificant link in the chain of creation would prove to be the vital one.

'After all, I can stand the loss,' he said aloud, surprising Mrs Griggs, who had brought up his breakfast. He was not at all surprised when the Knights seemed to oppose withdrawal from the Hope Quest. They could see money in it; it was the only motive of the Grail Foundation's other trustees. Ever since Merlin had known him, Kowalski might as well have had dollar signs for eyes. My father and Hector Kowalski; a right pair, Merlin thought. Neither of them let sentiment run their lives. Neither should he.

Chapter 24

It was late when Tamara reached Cornwall. She stopped at a pub for the night, and ensured sleep by taking a strong sedative. She turned up at Arthur's Castle just as Big Mac was starting his morning shift.

'Come back, have you?' he said with an automatic, almost absent-minded leer.

'Don't ring through for a moment, I wanted to have a word with you,' she said.

He took his hands from the telephone and finished adjusting his uniform. 'Oh yes?' he said.

'About my boyfriend.'

'Done a runner, hasn't he?' the young man said, leering meaningfully.

'Why do you say that?'

'Cos he's got the fuzz on his tail, hasn't he? They was here all day yesterday. The boss was fit to bust but I had to let them in.'

'Did he come here then, that morning? The day before yesterday?'

'I already told the police all I know, and that's nothing. Zilch. Zero.'

'He was on his way here, you see. That's why I wondered . . .'

He was not an unpleasant looking man, in his early twenties, brawny and healthy, with small eyes and pads of flesh that showed how fat he would be when older. Now he looked tough and vigorous and not very intelligent. His responses were those acquired from a peer group in which young women had a few specific functions. He began a movement towards her that Tamara quelled with her chilly stare. He visibly changed his mind about what to say, and answered sulkily, 'Well, I didn't see him.'

'Were you on duty the day before yesterday?'

'Ben wanted to swap, didn't he. I'm doing mornings this week.'

'So you would have been bound to see Dr Hope if he had come?'

'That's right.'

'Is there another entrance? A back way into the castle?'

'Some security that would be, I don't think. If your bloke turned up I'd know, like I told the cops.'

Of course the police would have been looking for the owner of the blue Volvo. 'Did they want to speak to me?' Tamara said.

'You'd have to ask the Major about that. Nobody tells me nothing. All I am's the hired help round here.'

But there did not seem to be much point in repeating the official questions and, no doubt, meeting a repetition of the denials that the police had received and Tamara herself had already heard.

Mac had assumed that Alastair had 'done a runner'. Had he picked that up from the police too? The live-in companion, the significant other, of a woman who finds a dead body, disappears; presumably the police now supposed what Tamara was determined to disbelieve. Was a murder hunt going on for Alastair?

Tamara drove away from the entrance to Arthur's Castle, westwards along the coast road, the way that Alastair would have come as he drove from Buriton. She turned on the radio news and listened for an item that would run, police are trying to trace a man they wish to interview in connection with their enquiries into the death of Mrs Louise Waugh. It was not broadcast. But if the police were seeking him, they were in a better position to find him than Tamara was. If they had good cause for their suspicion, Tamara had no reason to want to find him.

Driving without much attention, Tamara reached the outskirts of Boscastle. Better fill up with petrol.

She queued to pay in the service station's shop. It was a grocery store, and several local people were standing around the till chatting to the proprietor, a middle-aged man with a strong Birmingham accent.

'We had the police in yesterday,' one woman, said. 'What are these new snacks like, Denny? Shall I try them? They were asking about the driver of that car, you know, the one that went over the cliff at Hell's Gate, poor thing, dreadful that was. Yes, and I'll have a couple of those harvest pies, too. Of course I didn't know anything, except I couldn't help noticing the helicopters, the noise was something awful. Here, if I give you the thirty-three pence you can give me a five pound note.'

'I heard it was something to do with that lot up at Arthur's Castle,' a very old Cornishman said. He spent several moments propping himself on his walking frame, to free a hand for his newspaper, the local one on whose front page was a dramatic photograph of the Volvo dangling at a perverse angle at the end of the helicopter's cables, with water pouring down from it. 'Foreigners, they are.'

'So am I, Jack. You've been telling me for the last twenty years that I've hardly been in the county five minutes.'

Jack said, 'That doesn't make you a local, mind, but at least you know what's what.'

'I told the policeman so yesterday. I saw the driver of that car,' the man said. He leant over to pick the right coins from the old man's hand. 'He came in for a fill-up.'

'Really?' The woman customer paused in her price comparison of the various bottled mineral waters stacked up by the door. 'Honestly? What was he like?'

'Can I help you miss? Which pump was it again?'

'I'm just getting one or two other things while I'm here,' Tamara said, putting some tins of fruit at random into a wire basket.

'Take your time. No hurry.'

'Go on, Denny, tell us about it.'

'Not much to say. I wouldn't have taken any notice except that I happened to admire the car, I know what they cost, those things. Tall, dark and handsome, you'd have called him, Maudie.'

'What did he say?'

'I don't know that he said anything. Gave me the money for a fill-up and some tobacco and went on his way.'

'Too busy planning his dreadful deed.'

'You wouldn't fill your car right up if you were planning to drive over the nearest cliff,' Denny said. 'That's what I said to the policewoman. Take my word for it, I said, you see life in this job, I know what I'm talking about. That man wasn't suicidal. That car went over by accident.'

Tamara paid for her petrol and some useless food and went out to her car. Alastair had got this far on his way from Buriton, and filled his gas-guzzling monster right up. The man was right, nobody would bother to do that who had any thought of its imminent destruction. And if he was getting away without her, or, for that matter, from her, he would not have been on this road in the first place, a long and inconvenient way from any fast route out of the peninsula.

So in the fifteen miles between here and Arthur's Castle, in the half hour it would take to travel between the two, something had happened.

Tamara set off to retrace her journey eastwards.

At the end of a bleak winter the hedges were still bare, the fields still that dingy monochrome they become after lying under snow. But spring flowers were beginning to poke through the undergrowth and where the road came close to the uncultivated cliff top bright patches of gorse shivered in the wind. Occasionally there were glimpses of the sea beyond, brilliantly peacock coloured in the intermittent sunshine.

What a beautiful day. Tamara felt as though a weight of depression had slid from her back.

'I never meant to hurt him.'

It was one of Alastair's increasingly rare intervals of lucidity, and for a moment he wondered what someone had meant to do, in bashing him over the head and tying him up in the dark.

'He's got to keep quiet now.'

A sudden, multiplied agony. Darkness.

The next time he came round his circumstances had changed. Someone had loosened the cruel bonds, though he was not free. Someone had washed him and changed his clothes. He was lying on a softer surface and was covered with a blanket. The gag on which his teeth had been clenched before was gone. Above all, his head was no longer in the muffling folds of a stinking hood.

A torch was aimed at his face. He could see nothing except the painful light, and tried to move his hand in front of his eyes, but found that he had not the strength to lift it.

'Keep quiet. Don't make a sound. I've got a gag ready if you do.'

Alastair's throat was dry and aching and he could not have spoken. At the croak he emitted, the shadowy figure behind the light lunged forward, but stopped and drew back when the sound ceased.

Alastair framed his lips to ask for a drink.

'Here.' A can was held to his mouth and he managed to swallow some fizzy liquid. It was a blessed relief but stung, and he shook his head feebly, repeating the movement as a sandwich was held towards him.

'I'll get you some water next time. But you'll have to wait.' The hand descended towards his face again. A piece of sticking plaster was slapped across his eyes, another over his open mouth. 'Sorry about that. But you've got to keep quiet.'

Tamara drove slowly. The road led through well-farmed countryside and the occasional village. Where had Alastair stopped – or been stopped?

She pulled over into a lay-by, furnished for holiday-makers' summer picnics with immovable, vandal-proof benches and tables, to consult the large-scale Ordnance Survey Map.

He could have turned off the road at several side roads, lanes or private drives. Would the police have bothered to do house-to-house checks on them all? But the last three miles of the road leading to Arthur's Castle were uninterrupted. Tamara pressed on, not knowing what she was looking for but hoping that she would know it when she saw it.

A couple of miles short of Arthur's Castle, a turning towards the sea, not marked on the map, led into an informal and probably illicit camp site, where battered vans and tattered tents rocked in the sharp wind. The ground surface was churned into mud. Tamara paused to look in. Several women, with wild hair and inadequate looking clothes, were at work by a long trestle table preparing food. Some children hung around their knees, others scuffled in the dirt at their feet. Further away, sitting on old bus and car seats around a fire, the men were smoking and settling the affairs of the world. The hot, exotic beat of reggae music thundered out over the incongruous landscape. Two women crouched beside a stack of poles. One was marked in equal sections of white and red paint. The women were trying clumsily to attach the multicoloured fabric of a tepee-shaped shelter to its blunt end. As Tamara watched, the wind shook the stuff from their hands and the pole fell to the ground.

Tamara got out of her car. She was wearing jeans and a fringed jacket made of soft yellow suede. Only someone experienced in pricing clothes at a glance would have realised the dramatic difference between her denim and leather, and that of the campers.

'Hey!'

'Sorry.'

'What do you want?' The speaker, panting and flushed, was wearing jeans too, though torn, with a wide-necked, embroidered, peasant-style blouse, over which she clutched a matted fun-fur jacket with one hand while she held her red hair off her face with the other.

Tamara guessed which orthodoxy was in force here. She said, 'I have been brought here. I have problems.'

As though it was a response prescribed by dogma, the girl said, 'This is the place to find all the answers.'

Chapter 25

The men were whispering. Outside the hut someone was groaning.

They had branded his face and throat.

Now he was an initiate too. Now he would never get away from the People.

'Inconvenient if he dies.'

Alastair tried to say that he was alive, but his stiff lips and tongue could not shape the words.

Another voice murmured, 'He's coming round. I'd better make sure he doesn't . . .' A soft cloth descended over his eyes and was tied behind his head.

'Here, give him a drink.'

He sucked greedily at the water, paused and drank again.

'Listen. I'm going to untie you. But don't try to do anything, just stay where you are. OK?'

'He'll have to be cleaned up, the stink is unbearable.'

Alastair was ashamed to stink. He tried to cooperate as his limbs were lifted and wiped, and a pan slid underneath him.

'You're good at this,' the first voice said.

'Do you think he needs some medication? He's burning hot.'

Alastair tried to frame the word. Penicillin. Antibiotic. He was the doctor. He knew what he needed.

'He'll have to do without.'

'But he might die.'

'Not this time. Not yet.'

This time he slept more easily. The People came back to him, but even as he dreamed of them he knew it was a dream. He had been tied again, gagged and blindfolded too, but he could turn and toss about on the sweaty Lilo. In its way, he thought when he woke, this is rest and sleep. I shall recover.

They had brought him yoghurt and some fruit juice.

'He seems better.' The whisper was familiar. It had come to him in his dreams as the voice of the Old Woman. But this was a man. Alastair felt his wool-clad arm against his face.

'Do you think we can talk to him then?'

'Later. You have got to keep quiet, do you understand? Nod. That's right. Can you whisper?'

'A bit.' It hurt to say even that much. They need not expect him to shout for help.

'All right, prop him up a bit. Let me just . . .' The men had brought other equipment with them this time. They dressed Alastair in a homemade strait-jacket, a tough, long garment that fitted closely around him and was fastened at the back. His arms were held under the fabric to his sides. Even if he had the strength to try, he did not think he would be able to burst his way out of it.

Alastair muttered, 'Can't you tell me what all this is about?'

'We'll talk later. I'm coming back tonight.'

'What day is it?'

The man slapped plaster on to Alastair's raw lips. He grunted and winced. The hood was pulled down over his head. Darkness.

'Sorry but we have got to be sure you won't make any noise. See you later.'

Alastair told himself that he had to regain his strength if he was ever to deal with his captors. He thought he should be able to deal with them. They were not brutal, he thought. They did not want him to die.

His temperature was down, but he was as weak as a baby.

I've got the shaking fever, malaria. The symptoms will come back.

Sleep and rest, he thought, that's what the doctor orders; and for a little while managed to doze. But he was not in the conditions any doctor would prescribe. He tried to edge the blindfold slightly upwards by rubbing it against his upper arm, but he could not see anything at all, not the slightest gleam of light. It was very cold, with a dank, damp chill in the air and a biting draught. He listened attentively for a long time, restraining his own hoarse breathing as he tried to catch some clue as to his whereabouts.

He could hear nothing except what sounded like the intermittent dripping of water on to a hard floor. Could he be in an outhouse somewhere, with a sink? Had he dreamt the sound of the sea? Had he dreamt hearing Tamara? But they had moved him. This was a different place.

At least he was in England. Otherwise, he could not imagine what his prison was, or how long he had been in it. It must be a couple of days at least, long enough to give way to an acute fever and to be getting better. Although weak, he was at least making sense.

What had happened? Where was Tamara? She had sneezed, close by. Tamara . . .

He had been driving, he remembered that; driving where? why? For the time being he had no idea, and when he tried to force his brain into remembering was repeatedly distracted by physical misery. Two or three times he heard the groaning noise that had seemed to be the elders outside the Private Hut, when he imagined himself back with the People.

He was almost as bored as he was uncomfortable.

Uncomfortable.

I'll never use that word about a patient again, he thought, remembering his own voice uttering the inadequate adjective to a sufferer's relatives. I'm in agony. My patients were in agony.

Think about something else.

What was he here for? What was the object of the exercise?

A ransom demand? Ridiculous. He had no money. His father was a National Health Service General Practitioner with a small list and a large area to cover; his mother was a primary school teacher. They had no capital at all.

'What's so special about me?' Alastair Hope thought. 'Why me?'

'I am afraid that you cannot have it both ways,' Keith Hardman said. He was the very model of the modern city solicitor, and could have been mistaken for an international banker, a business tycoon or a newspaper proprietor. He earned as much as all but his very richest clients and enjoyed the same relaxations. His profession had come a long way since humble attorneys visiting their clients came to the back door and were given their meals in the housekeeper's room; Wootton Hardman had come a long way since it was a small, reliable, low-profile family firm. Still using the name of the two original partners, it now had fifty-three; still with an address in the shadow of the Bank of England, it now occupied a tower block in London and several floors of offices in New York, Paris, Hong Kong and Bonn. Expansion, modernisation and money had not, however, changed the essential qualifications of a good lawyer. He had listened carefully to Merlin Lloyd, and his opinion was unequivocal.

'When the Grail Foundation was established you surrendered your personal right to control its funds. The money is no longer your own,' he told Merlin Lloyd. 'As you accepted at the time – I have a contemporary note of our conversation here – you have one vote. It does not outweigh the votes of the other trustees.'

Merlin swung his chair away from his visitor, so as to stare out of his glass wall towards the sea. Ready tears, rising as often from irritation or frustration as from grief, were a purely physical symptom of his condition, but he had never stopped being embarrassed by what he had been brought up to think a sign of weakness. He blew his nose loudly, and made a practised sweep of the handkerchief across his eyes before turning back to the lawyer.

'It is a question of the terms of the settlement,' he said.

'They were drawn very widely indeed as you instructed. You did not want the Foundation to be restricted in its use of the funds. At the time you mentioned pettifogging legal niggles, I believe.'

'All the same, there must be some way to stop the other trustees perverting its aims.'

Keith Hardman in his turn moved over to the window. 'Fantastic view,' he said absently. 'I suppose that must be Lundy Island in the distance.'

'You can see a long way on clear days.'

'It's an amazing place. I'm glad to have a chance to see it after hearing so much about it. Quite a contrast for you after Australia.'

Not such a contrast as you are yourself, Merlin Lloyd thought, comparing the dapper figure before him with the memory of his lawyer from Melbourne, a smart operator who presented himself in the disguise of a simple country boy from the outback. He said, 'Is there some way I can get rid of the original trustees?'

'I beg your pardon? It's not easy to concentrate with that distracting view out there. I don't think I quite grasp what the point at issue really is. As far as I can see from these accounts the Foundation is doing very well. And the list of projects funded seems to be fully in conformity with your original aims.'

'Quests, we call them.'

'Yes, the Arthurian connection. Perhaps I didn't quite understand it. I was under the impression that the words were used symbolically rather than literally.'

'That is a way of looking at it. The symbol is of an ideal, an attitude of mind, a way of behaving that I was hoping to revive, even, if you like, a last stand for civilisation. It's not just another way of getting rich. And above all it's not to be used for turning us into barbarians ourselves.'

'Perhaps that's putting it a little strongly,' Keith Hardman said. 'Making use of the information brought back by the Hope expedition would be perfectly proper and in accordance with the trust's articles.'

'How would we differ from the barbarians who ended the kingdom of Arthur if we destroyed another society for our own profit?' Merlin asked.

'Would it necessarily be destruction?' Hardman protested. 'Surely it's a question of extending scientific understanding, exactly as it is expressed here, let me see, in clause thirty-one, subsection four, shall I read it?'

'I know the paragraph you refer to. But we are not talking about adding to knowledge here. Kowalski and Blair just want to get rich,' Merlin said. 'It was you who suggested appointing them, now I come to think of it.'

The lawyer said coldly, 'As far as I recall I advised that the Foundation should have trustees of good standing and with international connections and you agreed at the time. It was very fully discussed between your Australian representatives and ourselves.

Would you like me to send you an aide-mémoire of what was said?'

'I can remember perfectly, thank you,' Merlin said.

'Of course there is an argument that if the Foundation carries on with the work, it has some control over what happens next. The cat's out of the bag now. If you don't carry on, someone else will. Your young emissary came up with the Grail and a lot of people will want to get their hands on it.'

'Of course, at the moment,' Merlin said, 'that depends on getting their hands on the elusive Alastair Hope.'

He was special because of the People.

'You have got to tell me about it,' the man hissed.

He had come after a long time, too long a time, so that Alastair began to babble and weep when his eyes were untied and he saw a gleam of light, but he managed to pull himself together after eating a piece of pastry with some vegetables baked in it and drinking from two of those little cardboard containers of orange juice, and after he had been allowed to stagger into a corner of the room to relieve himself. It was as much as he could do to stay on his feet. He held himself against the wall. It was stone, rough and jagged edged, and slimy.

He did not want to go back to the Lilo but he was too weak to stand after being immobilised for so long. He managed to prop himself against the wall, and sat facing his captor.

The light was very dim. He could not see clearly. He stared, bemused for a while until he realised that the man had a stocking mask over his face and an anorak hood tied closely around it.

He thought that there had been two men before, one stout, one thinner, neither as ruthless as they would be if they were professional kidnappers. Didn't he remember one of them actually apologising? Perhaps this one would crumble if Alastair had the strength to oppose him. But the received wisdom was to mollify aggressors. There had been a lecture about it at medical school. The soft answer turneth away wrath.

The man hunkered down, resting a knife on his knee. 'I don't want to hurt you, but I will if I have to,' he said in a whisper muffled by fabric. Alastair was suddenly not even certain that it was a man.

'What do you want me to do? What do you want?'

'Keep your voice down.'

Alastair said, 'If you would only tell me what all this is about.' The face seemed to be turned towards him, nightmarishly amorphous, waiting, watching. Alastair said urgently, though still in a hoarse whisper, 'Come on for Christ's sake. You must have had some reason for abducting me. I can tell you straight off that I haven't got any money or access to any either. There's nobody will pay a ransom for me.'

'You have got something I want.'

'You've got the wrong man. I haven't got anything.'

'The information about El Dorado and the whereabouts of the People. That's what we want you to give us.'

'What the hell are you talking about?'

'Sssh. Keep your voice down. You know damn well what I mean. You'll tell me and then I'll let you go.'

'No.'

The other man lifted the knife. Its blade gleamed in the dim light. He said, 'Now let's begin.'

Chapter 26

A small child squatted down in front of a tent. He was wearing muddy dungarees, with a tear in the fabric which exposed his bottom. He crapped on the beaten earth, as many dogs had already done elsewhere in the encampment.

Tamara tried not to look judgemental. The child's mother glanced at her without apology. 'We believe in natural behaviour here.'

'It . . . I suppose it's a good fertiliser,' Tamara said.

'Right,' the other woman cried enthusiastically.

'A form of symbiosis. Returning to the earth what has come from the earth,' Tamara went on, warming to the theme.

The child's mother gently removed his hands from tearing at the skin of his bottom. It was raw from scratching, with greenish scabs and oozing lesions that ran up his back and down his thighs.

'That looks sore,' Tamara said.

'I know, it's worms, he scratches in his sleep. We'll get Justinian to lay hands on it, won't we, Nelson?'

'You don't think the doctor or health visitor . . .'

'Poison him with chemicals? What do you think I am?' The young woman scooped her son defensively into her embrace. 'Come to that, who are you? What do you want? Are you a reporter?'

'No, of course not, I'm a traveller. I've come from Glastonbury, and before that I was in Herefordshire.'

'Well, you'll have to talk to Justinian. It's up to him, who comes here.'

'Is he the leader?'

'We don't believe in leaders, we're anti-hierarchical. But Justinian always knows.'

'Is he somewhere around? I'd like to see him.'

'Roc!' The woman screeched like a bird, and a man shambled towards her carrying an enamel mug in which a pinkish liquid steamed in the chilly air. A couple of the skinny mongrels that prowled around the area came at his heel.

'Justinian went off with Ben last night again. I'll show you round.' Less hostile than the woman, he seemed to appreciate the way Tamara looked, and rubbed a piece of the yellow suede of her jacket between finger and thumb. Tamara restrained herself from glancing down at the stain he must have left on it, and listened with apparent attention as he told her about the regular workshops with the Oak Dragon and its unruly daughter Rainbow Circle, the music and story-telling, the dancing, chanting and meditating that filled the community's days.

They walked past the table where the women were preparing food, a large enamel basin of brownish vegetable substances. They looked tired and chilly. Most had poor complexions and prominent chilblains on their fingers and toes. Roc himself sneezed regularly, wiping his nose on a dirty rag that he pulled from his sleeve.

'It's a healthy place here,' he said solemnly. 'I was at Glastonbury myself for a while. I don't remember you there. But this is better, with the sea so close. You can really get in touch with the elementals.'

It was very cold on this stretch of flat cliff top. The wind blowing straight in from the north brought moisture on it, slightly salt even three hundred feet above the sea. Tamara licked her lips to taste it.

The men at the fire were passing a bottle between them. 'Firewater, want some?' offered a man with a lot of bronze and turquoise amulets on leather thongs round his neck. She pretended to sip it. 'I saw you at Stonehenge last solstice, didn't I?'

'I was there the year before. This time I celebrated at Callanish.'

'The Hebrides. Great. I was there two years ago.'

'Do you need help with your bender?' Roc said.

'Martha won't like it,' one of his friends warned.

'I'm free aren't I?' Roc said.

'In a minute, thanks,' Tamara said. She walked casually towards the women working on their tepee. They had managed to tie the frame together, a bunch of varied long sticks, but they were making heavy weather of getting the unsuitable fabric to stay on top. The red and white pole was smooth and exotic compared with the rough branches.

'Let me help,' Tamara said. She squatted down and held the striped pole steady while the other women struggled with the billowing canvas. Both of them had bad breath and smelt powerfully of blood and sweat. Almost imperceptibly Tamara turned the ranging pole round. It was standard issue but her own initials were painted very small on the bottom stripe.

'You've come to join us?' The voice was pleasant, even welcoming, but it struck Tamara with a sudden chill.

'Justinian, you're back! We missed you so much.' Women, men, children and dogs all clustered around the newcomer.

Tamara turned and stood, to meet his eyes. They were clear, bright, small pupilled, with whites almost as blue as the irises. They stared with concentration into her own.

Unlike the other campers, Justinian was perfectly clean, smoothly shaved and had hair that was not just cut but well cut. He was tall and firmly fat, as though the bulging skin would be hard to touch. His expression was mild and wondering, with the all-seeing gentleness that was the trademark of New Age inspirationists. Tamara recognised it, having seen it in the faces of numerous visitors to archaeological sites who knew, they said, what scientists could only guess.

Even without hearing his arguments, Tamara recognised that Justinian could influence others. Some, she supposed, he hypnotised or charmed, in the original sense of the word. Herself exceptionally immune to charismatic persuasion, she could see that some people would come under his influence; but she still wondered why such submission also entailed condemnation to the mediaeval discomfort of this cliff-top camp and deprivation of the benefits of modern medicine and conveniences.

Tamara, incapable of belief herself, sometimes regretted that she had been born incredulous, and under Justinian's blue regard, briefly (but only briefly) found herself surrendering her will to his. Switching her awareness into battle station, she smiled with sweet artifice.

She was about to begin her spiel about Glastonbury and camp-points north, when Justinian said,

'Tamara.'

'Yes, I am, how did you know?'

'I was expecting you.'

'You were . . . but how? Why?'

'Your friend was here the day before yesterday.'

She felt an excited warmth rising in her cheeks. 'Alastair was here? That means—'

'She's called Thea.'

'Oh. Thea Crawford. Of course.'

'It's over here. Manfred and Helge will show you.'

Manfred and Helge were huge, young and delighted with themselves. They had visited eight camps in Albion, they said, travelling from Wales to Somerset, from Ireland to East Anglia, in their conviction that somewhere they would find a symbol of enlightenment. And here, in Cornwall, they had come upon it. Manfred had been digging the gash-pit, and in it lay their sign. It was a stone head, consisting of a granite boulder, on which a life-size face was carved in bas relief, with full lips, oval beard and large eyes, the pupils indicated by round indentations in the rough stone.

The treasure trove was lying in a nest of grass and leaves.

'It is a message from the Celtic past,' Manfred said.

'From Arthur himself!' Helge breathed.

'What did Thea Crawford say it is?' Tamara asked.

'She chose to think it a modern fake,' Justinian said, laughing gently.

'Ah,' Tamara sighed, glad to have her own immediate reaction confirmed. 'I didn't think there were any Celtic heads like that.'

'She's wrong, as it happens.' Justinian put his long, well-manicured fingers on the face.

'Justin has the eye that can see. He knows,' said a girl who trailed his footsteps silently.

'Fake or not, your friend took a reel of photographs. She left her measuring scale behind. The women are using it as a tent pole.'

'She would probably say they are welcome to it,' Tamara said.

'As you are welcome to have seen our treasure,' Justinian said gravely.

'That's not really what I came for. I was wondering whether you had seen my friend. He might have come this way a couple of days ago. A man of my age, dark and—'

'You are speaking of Alastair.'

'Alastair Hope, yes.'

'We do not use surnames here. But Alastair died,' Justinian said compassionately. 'He did not come here, but we heard what happened to him. His car went over the cliff into the sea. You will never find him now.'

Chapter 27

Thea Crawford, who read only what Sylvester marked for her in the newspapers, and when he was away read none of them, but kept the daily four that were delivered to the house in ever-growing stacks in the laundry room for his return, heard belatedly about what had happened to Alastair's car on a local weekly news round-up programme. She had it on while making up her face. Her fingers slackened in their circular movement, and she stared unseeing at the blob of cream on her cheek.

Tamara's young man dead!

I can't believe it, it's not possible.

When did it happen?

Thea went to the telephone and left a message on Tamara's machine in the London flat and then failed to reach Sylvester, who should have been in Atlanta, Georgia, as far as she could make out from the schedule the television company had provided.

She went downstairs, scooping the papers from the mat on her way into the kitchen. Only the local one had any mention of Alastair Hope, and Thea read carefully through its account. The accident seemed to have happened two days before. She had been up in north Cornwall herself.

She went up to finish dressing and painting her face. She studied her full-length reflection with practised but cursory concentration, before returning her attention to the other day. Not far from that camp site, as the crow flies, Alastair's navy Volvo had plunged to destruction. On the camp site, two evenings before, Thea had seen the wing of a dark blue car under an inefficient cover.

She went down the stairs and picked her car keys out of the bowl on the hall table. Then she put them down and went back to the telephone. There was unlikely to be any connection, she supposed, between Louise Waugh's death and this awful accident, but none the less, when she got through to the police station, she asked to speak to WPC Parkin.

I wonder how Tamara would get herself out of this, Alastair Hope thought, flexing his muscles yet one more time against the fabric that tethered him.

With one bound our heroine was free. She would be, too. He had no doubt that she could work out how to escape, and would have escaped long since.

Alastair had been told by Clovis Crawford about Tamara's unusual attributes. Clovis was not supposed to know, of course, any more than his father Sylvester was. Like so much else in the world of journalists, it was part of the territory of nods and winks, of 'being in the know', of hearing all and saying little. Even Sylvester, dedicated to discovering and broadcasting the news, was the keeper of much information that he regarded as unpublishable.

'I don't go in for that kind of establishment hypocrisy,' Clovis had said. 'They keep secrets from the citizen. Any so-called enemy has been told everything already.'

'By people like you?' asked Alastair, who was rather shocked by his friend's indiscretion.

'Not unless you are the enemy,' Clovis replied, who knew that he was not, being one of Alastair's best friends since Cambridge days and sympathetic about his fascination for Tamara Hoyland. 'This is something you need to know.'

It had shaken Alastair to think of her as some kind of James Bond and the idea cast a shadow over their intimacy at first, but Tamara's disguise was impenetrable and beguiling, and quite soon Alastair ceased to think about what lay beneath it. She would tell him herself, in her own good time. Both, after all, had preserved certain privacies.

But Alastair felt inferior to her, which was not quite the same thing as admiring her, and was ashamed of his own pettiness when he analysed his discomfort. It was the injured pride of a male animal.

He would not feel any resentment at a woman's superiority in music or art. He ought to be glad of other esoteric qualifications. He decided that if she did not think him inadequate, he needn't.

But that was before he had any idea that he might have occasion to wish for such accomplishments himself. Restored to a condition that permitted consecutive thought, Alastair made a sober assessment of his own incapability.

He had no way of escape. He could not imagine even the most fantastic or least feasible method of getting away. He had no idea why he had been imprisoned, or by whom, or for how long. Nor did he have the faintest idea where he was.

No longer floundering, Tamara knew where she was going at last.

Alastair had stopped at the garage for petrol on the road from Buriton and then driven on towards Arthur's Castle. Someone from Justinian's encampment had taken the ranging pole from the boot of the car. Someone had driven the car a few miles up the coast to the sheer drop at Hell's Gate and pushed it over the cliff. Where was Alastair when that happened?

At Arthur's Castle. That was where he had to be, willingly or otherwise, from his own choice or held incommunicado by force.

She had not much to base this judgement on, but it was enough to be going on with, now that she had properly recalled and analysed the moment when she had stood inside the castle door, the darkening chill of early spring dusk behind her, the brilliant warmth of Merlin's fantasy ahead.

Major Griggs offered to take her coat. He put his hand on her lapel, ready to help her, and she had half turned, shaking her head, and looking towards the row of antlers where visitors put their outdoor clothes. A waxed cotton coat with corduroy collar hung there, the kind of waterproof jacket that hundreds of people had used ever since they were popularised by some member of the royal family and became the uniform gear of the country classes, and later copied by cheaper manufacturers and supplied by mass retailers.

Alastair had a coat like that. And as Tamara swung back to

say that she could not stay, she had smelt him – or his tobacco; it was his trademark, the invisible intimation that he was nearby. It clung to all his clothes. His pockets contained shreds of spilt tobacco and all the fabric had the same, familiar odour of smoke, perhaps because he had the habit of pushing the pipe, sometimes still smouldering, deep into a pocket before he came into the house.

Tamara had smelt the spicy, agreeable aroma without recognising it at the time, but she remembered that a quiver of pleasure disturbed her hard, angry determination to get away. But immediately the intellect had converted instinctive affection for the familiar, though unidentified, lover's smell into an unfocused fear and despair that had stayed with her the rest of the evening and night.

Yes, that had been Alastair's coat hanging beside a couple of anonymous fawn macintoshes and a fur-lined cape. That was what had niggled at her mind, the flaw in an otherwise impeccable performance. He had been back to Arthur's Castle.

Mr Black might have recognised a glint in Tamara's eye; her family might have been warned by a certain decisiveness of speech and movement that in childhood had presaged behaviour of which they were likely to disapprove. Tamara Hoyland was at work.

Chapter 28

The catering firm known as Pixy's Pantry had changed hands several times since being christened by its founder, an estate agent's wife who thought it would be fun to run her own business and soon found she was wrong. But she built up enough goodwill to make it worth selling the name. The present proprietor also owned some holiday chalets, a health club and three garages, and Pixy's Pantry was managed by a refugee from the health service dietetics department. The only reminder that it had been founded by a woman whose garden was full of plastic gnomes was a green figure with a red pointed cap painted on the vans that delivered the ready-cooked meals to their destinations.

The vans were fitted with heated compartments, ice boxes, plate racks and cutlery baskets. Food, dishes and silver were taken from Wadebridge to clients over a wide radius, some for special events, some as a regular, daily service.

The driver and the waitresses, already dressed in their gathered dresses, pinafores and mob caps, sat in the front. There was a rapid turnover of staff. Although customers paid dear for their convenient meals, the workforce received too small a proportion of the profits to be faithful, and even at the job centre a post with Pixy's Pantry was described as temporary.

The van came to Arthur's Castle twice a day, bringing luncheon and dinner. It was waved through the barrier at the entrance quite casually; its occupants were no longer counted in and out. They drove straight to the tramway where supplies and servers were transferred on to the little conveyance and into the castle. Usually Mrs Griggs was waiting to supervise the delivery and arrangement of the food. On the days that her husband stood by, he always checked the period details of the girls' clothes and lifted the lids to taste the contents.

The employees of Pixy's Pantry signed agreements about Arthur's Castle. They knew that they were not allowed to wander off the path from kitchen to great hall and back or to snoop or tell tales (a detail honoured in the breach rather than the observance) or take photographs. Major Griggs did his best to arrange that none would have the chance. He made sure that either he or his wife was on hand until the detritus of the meals and the used crockery and cutlery had been cleared and gone down in the lift again. On the way back to Wadebridge the girls usually dozed, exhausted by trotting to and fro in marble halls. None of them would have lived at Arthur's Castle for any money. Their first impression was of a magnificent film set but, as one of the students who had stuck it out for three days said, magnificence had always been hard on the skivvies who kept it so.

'Remember to tell the boss there's only three for meals after today,' one of the girls said.

'Is that what they said?'

'All the visitors are leaving first thing.'

'Taking a certain person along with them?' The three women in the van giggled in salacious unity.

'Funny, that, for nowadays. It's like really going back to the dark ages, having to be so secretive about sex.'

'I'm surprised they don't lay wenches on with the rations.'

'That Count behaves as if we were.'

'He's quite attractive still.'

'One night of love, eh? It hardly seems worth the effort.'

If the effort had been for a night of love, it would certainly not have been worth while. By the time that she could be reasonably sure that everyone had gone to bed Tamara Hoyland was cold, stiff, furiously bored and hungry. There was a larder stocked for a siege, as Tamara had found on her earlier night of exploration, but it was accessible only through the kitchen. The cupboard of emergency equipment, kept so as to render the castle independent of mains services in case of need, had not included anything to eat. She was squashed up against cylinders of bottled gas, cans of paraffin and shelves laden with candles, Aladdin lamps, methylated spirits, stacks of batteries in various sizes and of torches and flashlights, one of which Tamara put in her pocket. She waited, perched on one of the mobile gas heaters, which she padded with the discarded uniform of Pixy's Pantry.

She edged the door open. The lobby into which the tram platform opened was empty and silent. There was never daylight here. The flambeau-shaped lamps, designed to create a semblance of welcome, were dimmed.

One advantage of marble was that one could move on it silently. No doubt the concealed cameras were switched permanently on; but in the dim light Tamara did not think she would be recognisable on a screen. The building was not equipped with conventional burglar alarms, since it was presumably supposed to be impossible to enter at night. So she had no need to worry about heat-sensitive spy-eyes, or stepping on the wrong bit of floor pad.

Moving quickly and without undue caution Tamara crossed the solar, looking about her for changes since her last visit, but everything was tidied and impersonal. A row of coats hung on the antlers by the door, Sir Hector's dark with the regulation velvet collar, the Count's military style with epaulettes. There was an oblong lump in one of its pockets: a packet of photographs, the photographs of the unknown jungle city that Louise had brought to Arthur's Castle. Tamara put them back where she had found them. There were other copies. She took Alastair's coat from the rack and briefly pressed her face into its corduroy collar, sniffing up the reminder of his physical presence; smoke and lemon verbena and, for some reason, fish. A packet of tobacco was in one pocket, as well as some matches, an old biro and a crumpled piece of white paper printed with the words, 'Disposable glove. Remove plastic glove from backing paper. Shell makes the most of motoring.' The coral silk scarf was not there.

Tamara went up to the first floor. She listened outside the rooms that were occupied. Sir Hubert Blair was snoring so loudly that it could be heard through the thick door. The General was listening to the Voice of America. An excited woman was talking about a tribe of Stone Age people who had come out of the unexplored Brazilian jungle. 'A spokesperson for the National Fund for the Indians said they call themselves the People. They say they have come to get treatment for one of their number because they heard that the white man's medicine could cure him.'

The room known as Queen Guinevere had been tidied up since she left it the other morning. Tamara drank some fruit juice from the ice box hidden in a court cupboard.

In Sir Bedivere, a used shirt, a crumpled tie, a suit on a hanger, all showed that Alastair had intended to come back to Arthur's Castle.

Tamara put her finger on the toothbrush. Bone dry. She unscrewed the bottle of malaria pills. He had one more week's prophylaxis to swallow, to make him safe from any incubated infection. He was scrupulously careful about remembering it. Monday morning would have been his last dose. The tablet was still in the bottle.

He had not been here, then; at least, not in this room.

Tamara moved out into the passage and towards the stairs. Lord Collin was coming up them in his pyjamas without a dressing gown. He was carrying a full bottle of whisky. 'Dear girl,' he muttered, obviously embarrassed. 'Knock-out drops, you know. I couldn't sleep.'

'What a good idea,' Tamara said.

'They said you'd left, you and your young chap.'

'I came back again.'

'They said he'd cheated us. You going to make him change his mind?'

'I can try.'

'Join me for a drink?'

'That is kind of you. But I was just on my way to bed.'

'Sleep well then, my dear,' he said. 'See you in the morning.'

Tamara waited until he had gone into the room called Sir Kay. Perhaps she should simply go to bed herself, back in Queen Guinevere's room. Perhaps she was all wrong and Alastair was not here at all, and had not been here.

But Lord Collin might not have known. He was obviously a figurehead, not really involved with what went on in the Grail Foundation.

On up to the top floor. There were voices coming from behind the door, but the words were indistinguishable. Blessing the expensively solid work of Guyler and Ghosh, Tamara slowly twisted the door handle and pushed very slightly.

Three men, the deep, musical voice of Merlin Lloyd himself, Justinian's insinuating, light tone, and Ben Oriel's, immature, halting, husky.

'That's good,' Justinian said. 'Good news that you can stop the exploitation. Better news that you will send us to warn the people against the profit seekers and land rapists. We shall bring back such knowledge . . .' His voice was exalted. Merlin replied,

'I'm glad that Alastair Hope has told you where to go. But I need to talk to him myself.'

'We shall bring him to you, perhaps tomorrow. But we ought to—'

Tamara caught a valedictory tone and pulled the door silently to. She stepped behind a curtain drawn across the high window; by day this landing must be rainbow coloured from a stained-glass picture of a king and suppliant. She drew her feet up on to the window ledge, lest they showed beneath the velvet, but rightly doubted that either man would be observant. When they had gone down to the bend of the stairs she edged out and after them, following at a distance as they descended to the ground floor.

Justinian was wearing a transparent plastic cape. Ben Oriel had on a raincoat too. It was identical to Alastair's, to the waxed, proofed cotton with a corduroy collar and tartan lining that hung on that antler, impregnated with its smell of tobacco and of fish – the fish that had suffused Ben Oriel's van.

Ben Oriel had worn Alastair's coat when he drove Louise and Tamara to Buriton.

Ben said, 'So what do we do now? You shouldn't have told the old man that we'd bring—'

'Hush. Don't worry.'

'But what if—'

'Ben.' Justinian's voice was compelling and Ben lowered his hand and turned away. Like a sulky child he muttered,

'We'll have to think of something soon. It's been two days now.'

Justinian said, 'I promise you I know what to do. I am going to arrange it now, we shall need the others.'

'I don't—'

'They helped us before, remember. They do what I ask.'

Ben opened and closed the huge door for him, pushing it against the violence of the weather.

Tamara, standing with her back flat against the wall around the corner, watched his shadow reflected against the shiny marble.

Two days, Tamara thought. Two days since Alastair had disappeared?

Ben walked softly across the pretend-rushes and towards the passage that led to the tramway. He shut the door behind him. Giving him time to get out of sight, Tamara opened it to slip through after him.

He got into the little carriage and she heard the groan of machinery as it began to move slowly downwards.

The noise stopped too soon. Was it stuck? Tamara moved on to the platform. Leaning forwards, she peered down into the tunnel. The carriage was faintly illuminated; it was standing still, but she would not be able to see it from here at all if it had reached the bottom.

Ben Oriel had stopped it halfway down.

Alastair was waiting for them. He had heard the tram starting up and although he did not know what it was, he recognised the sound as presaging his captors' arrival. Would it be the thin or the fat one, or both?

It was the thin one. He tore the plaster from Alastair's lips and eyes. The pain was excruciating. It was a while before Alastair could say, 'I need to piss.'

His warder unbound the strait-jacket a little, not to free Alastair but to let him move his arms within it. He untied his feet, standing well out of range of any kick. Understanding too late, Alastair realised that kicking or struggling had not even occurred to him. Had he missed a chance to free himself, by his cowardly, passive, unmanly inertia? I deserve to be a victim, he thought. The man aimed the torch beam so that Alastair could see where to go. For the first time he took in that he was in some kind of stone cavern, its walls rough and un-dressed, the roof uneven and too low for him to stand upright.

Alastair shuffled across the rough floor, his feet crunching against the loose stones and obediently, passively relieved himself. He immediately felt more courageous. Urinary emergency as a cause of cowardice, he thought, as though it were the title of a scientific article, and turned towards the light.

One could short the whole system by throwing a metal bar across the live and inert rails. There were picks and shovels in the store cupboard. Tamara had turned to fetch one when she changed her mind. Better not to let Ben Oriel have any inkling that someone was coming. If he had killed once, he would not hesitate to do so again.

Tamara was wearing narrow trousers and a zipped, multi-pocketed jacket, fitted at wrist and waist with knitted bands. She bent to tuck the trouser bottoms into her socks and double knot the laces of her gym shoes. She tied her hair tightly into its velvet band.

For a moment she stood motionless, shining the light on the decorated walls of the sloping shaft and then on to the parallel rails. 'It's simply a question of keeping straight,' she told herself. She gripped the torch in her teeth and swung herself down into the shallow trench.

Tamara went down backwards, finding protuberances in the roughly chiselled floor to rest her hands and feet in proper rock-climbing style. Everything was wet and slippery. Water dripped continuously down. Tamara placed her toes carefully, keeping them in line like a dancer. She kept her shoulder pressed against the side wall, bumping from plastic stalagmite to incongruous wall painting. Her own panting breath sounded audibly against the echo of the tide from the beach below.

However cautiously she moved her hands and feet, one at a time, testing their grip, it was impossible to keep absolutely straight. Once she was pushed off balance and jerked towards the dangerous rail, but she balanced herself again and paused to calm herself. She was wet through, as much from sweat as from the drips of water. She wiped her forehead with the back of her arm; and while she was still, heard a sound from below.

How much further to go? With a cautious twist of her neck, Tamara managed to look backwards, down the shaft. She was past the point of no return. Onwards. She put the torch into her pocket and began to descend again, more quickly now, because if the tram began to come up while she was in the shaft . . . she averted her mind from everything except the immediate task.

Concentrate. Move a hand, move a foot, the other hand, the other foot, keep the wall rubbing against the hip and shoulder, slowly, carefully, more haste less speed . . .

Someone had climbed into the carriage. She heard the creaking of the springs. A voice said, 'Come on, damn you.'

Onwards. Hurry. Fifty feet.

Why hadn't he noticed her?

Fumbling sounds. A muffled ejaculation. 'I can't see, the light's in my eyes.' Alastair's voice, husky but unmistakable.

He would see her perfectly clearly if he looked now. The light within the little carriage cast Tamara's shadow in front of her, a grotesque bat-shape on the rough, wet rock.

Nearly there.

The blunt end of the gondola touched the back of Tamara's leg. She propelled herself backwards and around, so as to land kneeling on the slippery metal.

Her impact rocked the tram. Ben fell noisily against the seat.

'Tamara?'

It was Alastair.

'Keep back,' she snapped.

She saw the shape of a man scrambling upright, his hands outstretched towards her.

Ben Oriel, the security guard, had never learnt anything about attack or self-defence. Tamara had undergone extensive training, but it was a while ago and she had not practised since retiring from Department E.

She wished to immobilise him, that was all, but untrained or not, he was twice her size and young; and he had held Alastair a prisoner for nearly three days.

With her feints and passes, her ducking and weaving, did Tamara will the end result? Not consciously, not at the time, and if later doubts surfaced when she relived what had been an episode of no more than a minute, she never knew, never really knew, whether they were justified.

Ben Oriel lunged forward towards her. She stepped aside and

thrust her leg into his path. He fell forward, sprawling over the downhill slope of the little carriage, his stomach on the smooth metal, his fingers grasping out for a hand-hold that was not there, and with a hideous deliberation, his body slid over the back and down, hands first, on to the live electric rail.

Chapter 29

Justinian jogged along the cliff path in his cocoon of plastic. His training shoes hit the slippery grass with metronomically regular slapping noises, and as he moved a wet slick of hair rose and fell against his dripping forehead. 'Just what your pot needs, Joe boy,' he thought. Now that his parents were both dead, nobody addressed him by his given name, or even, probably, knew what it was. But when he was alone, when nobody needed the sustenance of his attention or the inspiration of his words, the solitary, solid man was not the Justinian his disciples knew, but Joe Farmer, the fat boy from Fife, the butcher's son who was teased by his contemporaries, failed exams, was left unpicked for teams and had a horrendous case of acne.

Now he was Justinian, the guide, philosopher and friend to so many needy souls. He had developed the innate powers unrecognised and unappreciated by schoolteachers or parents. He had made himself strong and healthy. He had learnt to exercise control.

Joe/Justinian did not think of his past very often. It was twenty years since he had sloughed it off like an old skin.

He did, nowadays, think about his future.

This winter, for the first time, he had woken in the mornings stiff and aching. The good body had failed him, producing chilblains and varicose veins. How much longer could he go on living as he did? But how could he ever change, dependent as he was on the erratic gifts of admirers?

Money. It was a thought revived by the Joe Farmer in him. It surfaced, unexpected, when Ben Oriel arrived babbling about the Hope Expedition, and what it had found and how anyone and everyone must be prevented from finding it again.

I need money, Joe realised then. Quite a lot of money.

Thinking what could never be said, Justinian had reached the camp site. He moved to climb the wall that separated it from the cliff path. The stone head was set up on a little natural pillar of rock, its gaze directed towards the campers. Justinian had brought it there himself, carrying it from Arthur's Castle wrapped inside a pullover and then in a couple of bin liners. He had thought it would be found sooner, but it was not too late to confirm to his flock that he had chosen a site that was sanctified by ancient powers. Justinian himself had no need of such props to his belief, but he was aware that sometimes his weaker brethren required them.

Looking down the field towards the settlement, Justinian saw that there were visitors. A white car had driven in and another was blocking the entrance gate. Blue lights flashed on top of them. Indistinguishable messages were pouring idiotically from rival radios.

Pigs. It was not unprecedented. The campers were intensely unpopular in the neighbourhood and automatically suspected of every theft and act of vandalism. Some had been questioned, fewer charged and none, so far, convicted. This time Justinian realised that the questions would be about something less routine than the latest break-in at the corner shop.

Moving smoothly and without hesitation, he wheeled around and climbed nimbly back over the wall. On the seaward side it was almost completely dark, but he knew the way and had no fear of mistaking the path for the edge of the cliff. He set off back towards Arthur's Castle.

Since the blue, hideous, deathly flash from the live rail, all the dim lights in the shaft had gone out. Tamara and Alastair sat on the Lilo, propped together against the wall. It was uncomfortable, but for Alastair less so than anything else in the last three days. Tamara had overcome her own reactive shudders. Guilt about Ben Oriel could come later. Remorse and shame for her lack of faith in Alastair must wait too.

They had to get out of here, but Alastair was in no state to climb the shaft, safe perhaps with the electricity fused, but steep and slippery. Soon Tamara would have to leave him, get up or down alone and fetch help. But for the moment he was clinging to her, febrile and still frightened. He had been here in the dark, tied, gagged, blindfolded, ill, for days. Now was the time to convey comfort. Tamara kept her warm, dry hand on Alastair's sweaty skin and she spoke calmly in her light, clear voice.

When the torch was switched off one could see nothing except a faint diminution of the inky darkness marking the entrance to the man-made cave. The tide was nearly high and the breakers, surging near the bottom of the shaft, echoed upwards.

For the moment, they preferred not to see. The body of Ben Oriel was too close, spreadeagled where it had fallen, rigid, fingers clawed, the head turned sideways showing the hideous rictus of the mouth, the staring, meaningless anguish of the eyes. Alastair, subject to the automatic compulsion on doctors, had moved to go to him, but Tamara easily held him back; too easily. He was painfully weak, shivering and feverish.

'He must be dead,' she had said gently.

'I didn't see . . . what happened?'

'I was trying to keep him away from you. He slipped and fell.'

'Who? Who is it?'

Alastair had never seen the features behind the stocking mask. It would not have meant very much to him if he had, for the uniformed security guard had not attracted his attention and they had never properly met.

'There was another man. One thin, one fat,' Alastair said.

'The other man is Justinian, at least that's what he calls himself. He's some kind of guru.'

Justinian and his friends, with Ben, had stopped Alastair's car on the way to Arthur's Castle. A group of people was bending over someone who was lying on the road with his shirt unbuttoned.

'It must have been Ben Oriel who rang to tell you to come back. He was the only one who knew where I had gone. He must have guessed you would follow me.'

'I had to stop, of course, someone needed medical help,' Alastair said. 'But I think they must have knocked me out. The next thing I knew I was in here, wherever here is.'

Tamara had to explain where they were, how she had come

and why Alastair had been brought here. 'They wanted to prevent you telling anyone where you had been. They killed Louise Waugh to stop her telling.'

Thinking aloud, Tamara worked out what must have happened that day.

Ben Oriel had overheard the quarrel between Louise and Alastair. He had come into the solar after Alastair was summoned to his audience with the Knights and left the castle with the two women, picking up Alastair's coat, identical to his own, on the way. Even if Tamara had not been in a state of tension and distress, she would not have got any whiff of tobacco because of the smell of fish in Ben's van. Tamara had a very acute sense of smell, she added.

Alastair said, 'I smell disgusting. You shouldn't come so close to me,' but his arm tightened weakly around her as he spoke.

After Ben dropped Tamara at Thea's house in Buriton, he must have driven back towards Louise's house, parked his recognisable van somewhere obscure and walked.

She would have let him in, and then . . . had he slipped her sleeping pills in her coffee? Perhaps she had taken them to calm herself down. Perhaps she was already asleep when he entered the house and took one of Louise's own kitchen knives, holding it in the thin polythene gloves he had picked up at the petrol station earlier on. He would have gone upstairs, and found her lying on the bed, passive and unresisting as he slit her arteries.

'If he overheard anything about Louise being on that anti-coagulating medication, he might have realised that she would bleed to death very quickly. He must have been listening when she was slagging you off about the expedition.'

'But why should he . . . ?'

'You said he wanted you to tell about the People.' Tamara stopped herself from adding, in parenthesis, what she had heard on the Voice of America. 'He obviously felt terribly strongly about them and was determined to stop Louise from going to the papers about it all. I talked to him a bit. He was very committed to his green ideals.'

'But murder . . .'

'And kidnap.' Tamara tightened her grasp on Alastair. 'And

trying to cast suspicion on you . . . wearing your coat, that smear of blood, your handkerchief . . . It was unforgivable.'

'But he was so young. And he's dead.'

'I may manage to feel sorry for him one day.'

On his way down the stairs, Ben Oriel must have noticed a smear of blood on his hand and wiped it on the piece of material, Tamara's scarf, that he found in the coat pocket. Knowing that it had no connection with himself, knowing, rather, that it would add to the suspicion of Alastair, if any doubt that it was suicide arose, he had thrown it carelessly aside before leaving the house. Then a quick drive back to Arthur's Castle, where he would have put Alastair's coat back; and meanwhile Alastair had gone off to Buriton in Ben's.

'I thought you had done it,' Tamara said. 'I am so ashamed.'

Alastair's voice was weak and husky. His fever was getting worse, Tamara thought. 'Louise accused me of killing Robert Waugh. Did you believe that too?'

'No,' Tamara said. 'But did you?'

'Not me. The People did.' Alastair was convulsed by weak, painful coughs. 'I couldn't stop them.'

'I must fetch—'

'Don't let go.'

'All right.'

'Robert went to one of their forbidden places. He broke a taboo. I'd warned him. He didn't believe it was that important to them and he was being paid to bring back precious stones, metals, elements. So they . . . I heard him screaming.'

A sound echoed outside in the shaft. Tamara freed her arm and said, 'Let me just look.'

The faintest diminution of the darkness below; dawn, at last. And upwards, where the shaft rose into the living rock, voices and lights. Tamara cupped her hands around her mouth and shouted. Then she flashed the torch on and off, on and off: SOS. An answering voice echoed down the tunnel.

She went back to Alastair. 'Help's coming,' she said, and put her arms around his shaking, hot body.

'Don't leave me.'

'No, I won't.'

'I left the People. They didn't want me to go, they thought

I had come to stay with them for ever. They thought I was someone else, someone they had been waiting for. They thought I had come to save them. And I've betrayed them instead.'

'How?'

'I gave in, Tamara, I said where they are. I can't . . .' He broke off, his teeth chattering uncontrollably.

'Hold on. It won't be long now.'

'The People call it shaking sickness . . . malaria, I suppose . . . they've got a treatment . . . go back . . . bring it home . . . I have to go back to the People.'

He drew in a deep breath and managed to bring himself under a kind of control. He said, 'But it's too late. The People will be found. It's all over.'

'Why, Alastair?'

'I told you, I couldn't hold out. That knife . . . I'm such a coward. You would have kept the secret. But I gave it all away.' Alastair began to cry, difficult, hoarse tears.

Voices could be heard giving instructions. Light was spreading from the rescuers' lamps into the fetid chamber where Alastair had been incarcerated.

Tamara went to its entrance. Men were climbing down the shaft.

The first to reach them was the Count, his teeth gleaming in a man-of-action's grin. He carried a torch and a revolver. He was in his element.

'I thought it might be you,' Tamara said.

He bent over the body. 'You thought I'd killed this man?' he snapped.

'I thought you might have abducted Alastair and killed Louise Dench.'

'Why?'

'Because you were in Buriton the day she died, for one thing.'

'She mightn't have died at all if I'd managed to find her.' He stepped up on to the platform beside Tamara. 'Bad show,' he said, looking dispassionately at Alastair. 'Wounded, I suppose. Fine old mess all round.'

'Why didn't you see Louise that day?'

'None of the students I asked seemed to know where she lived. Not in the directory, nobody of her name at all.'

'She was called Waugh in private life. Didn't you know that she and Robert were married?'

'No I did not, and if she was married why was she called by a different name? Damned silly feminist nonsense. Here, take the other side, we'll get Hope into the tram.'

'If you never saw her that day, where did you get the packet of photographs?'

'The anthropologist still had a set, chap called Yule. The students I spoke to knew all about him, one of them took me straight there, no problem.'

Down below, where the shaft came out on to the beach, the police had come. A blue, flashing illumination moved regularly, eerily, over the body of Ben Oriel. Angular, inhuman, it lay head downwards across the rails. Some pieces of card had fallen from its jacket pocket, sliding and scattering below: the pictures of a city lost and found.

In the fitful glare, movement could be perceived overhead, near the curved, carved roof of the tunnel. At first Tamara could not see what it was, and then she recognised the dark, erratic shapes of bats.

Epilogue

From *The Cornish Observer*, Thursday, 4 April

DEATH OF SECURITY GUARD

A man who died when he fell on to a live electric rail had been reminded of its danger only a month before, the North Cornwall Coroner was told on Tuesday. An inquest heard that Benedict Alexander Oriel, 24, a security guard at Arthur's Castle, attended regular refresher courses on safety procedures. The Coroner recorded a verdict of accidental death coupled with a recommendation that the Health and Safety Officer should consider further measures to prevent access to the lift shaft.

From *The Cornish Observer*, Thursday, 11 April

Campers wept as their homes were removed last week when bulldozers were brought in by North Cornwall District Council to clear a cliff-top site of unauthorised tents and shelters. The Enforcement Officer said that the camp constituted a health hazard. Councillors were told that neighbours had complained of noise, litter and rats coming from the site.

From *The Western Morning News*, Saturday, 8 July

Property Update

Newly on the market in North Cornwall, Arthur's Castle is described by the agents as a luxurious cliff-top residence with spectacular views. Offers in excess of a million pounds are expected for a property with scope for conversion into a conference centre, country club or hotel. Outline planning permission has been granted for residential development on ninety-four acres of scrub land.

From *The Journal of Survival International*, Autumn edition

A new threat to the self-determination of Indians in North Western Brazil comes from the Grail Foundation's purchase of a two-hundred-square-mile area of the rainforest. The trustees, who include former MP Count Hector Kowalski and Australian millionaire Merlin Lloyd, plan to build a Centre of Alternative Wisdom, complete with museum, interpretation centre, theme park and accommodation for several hundred visitors. Letters protesting against the scheme should be sent now.

From Camisis Tours Brochure

Our exciting tour of the Amazon and rainforest area of Brazil will be accompanied by Baron Carl von Reiss. See the jungle before tree felling and mining destroy what is left of this great natural resource. Marvel at its richness of flora and fauna. Join in the spectacular rituals of the native dances. Two departures next year, in April and May.

From *The Cornish Observer*, Thursday, 9 November

The involvement of a middle-aged man in a cowardly attempt at kidnap and blackmail was described as 'a despicable offence' by Judge Jones at Truro Crown Court last week. He sentenced Joseph Harold Farmer (44) of The House of The New Age, Land's End, West Cornwall, to four years imprisonment for his part in a conspiracy to assault and falsely imprison Dr A J Hope of Edinburgh. 'Society must be kept safe from men like you,' the Judge told Farmer.

Three women who made a disturbance in the public gallery are to face charges of Contempt of Court.

From *Gillian's Journal*, in *Glossy Gossip*, December edition

On one gloriously sunny and crisp autumn Saturday I motored down to a charming country church in South Devon for the twelve noon marriage of Dr Alastair Hope, only son of Dr Jarndyce Hope of Inverneill, Argyll, and Miss Tamara Anastasia Anne Hoyland, younger daughter of Mr and Mrs Robert Hoyland of Cresscombe. There were lovely flowers arranged all over the church. The bride, who is a very pretty and clever girl, is the granddaughter of my old friend the late Countess Losinska who was one of the ladies-in-waiting of the last Tsarina of Russia, and was later to make a dramatic escape through Mongolia and Japan to safety.

The bride, who wore white lace with her dear grandmother's diamond tiara, was given away by her father and attended by her nieces. At the reception in the bride's home after the ceremony, I saw . . .

From *Fifty Years An Anthropologist*, the Memoirs of Professor Homer F Krebs

. . . always calls for the utmost delicacy in approach. A sad instance of what I have called 'the unwanted recoil syndrome' came my way just before this book went to press.

A young scholar at a British University, himself a medical man with a special interest in pharmacology, led an expedition to the Brazilian jungle, the aim being to research aboriginal herbal remedies and, incidentally, to provide the expedition's sponsors with new and commercially profitable plant products.

In due course Dr H (as I will call him) and his colleagues reached a remote point in a minimum-contact zone, where they encountered by chance one of the numerous unrecorded tribal groups of the Upper Amazon Basin.

Unfortunately neither medicos nor missionaries ever receive even elementary anthropological training and the inevitable outcome was that Dr H blundered into a reciprocity scenario of his own making. In return for treating minor wounds, lesions, chronic muscular conditions and the like, Dr H was made privy to some of the jungle pharmacopoeia.

On return to the United Kingdom, he evidently underwent a conversion to the ideal of the Noble Savage and forfeited the further support of his commercial sponsors by refusing to divulge the whereabouts of the tribe in question, on the grounds that any further exposure to civilisation would not only hasten their downfall, but also expunge the precious knowledge hitherto maintained in the secrecy of their remote habitat.

A year or so later, on honeymoon in Amazonia, Dr H and his bride entered a restaurant of the kind catering for tourists and normally, as my readers will know only too well, the haunt of diseased beggars at the side entrances, mendicant children hustling round the tables and picturesque aborigines performing the inevitable travesty of 'native dances' that is invariably presented as folklore.

Imagine Dr H's dismay when he recognised the dancers as members of the very tribe whose continued isolation he had sacrificed so much to ensure. Dr H's brief visit to them, while hardly an example of a cargo cult (see Appendix IV) had, unknown to him, constituted a Messiah Episode. Readers will recall a compelling example from New Guinea of the same from my earlier volume of memoirs, *Forty Years an Anthropologist*, in which I described how, following some fleeting contact decades earlier with a wandering medical missionary, the re-appearance of The White Saviour Who Cures became firmly embedded in tribal lore.

Dr H's protégés had, with little difficulty, traced his returning footsteps and followed in them with those of their number who, they supposed, could be cured by his ministrations. Within a matter of weeks they were ensnared in the very civilisation from which Dr H had been so anxious to protect them.

As we all know, the road to hell is paved with good intentions. Dr H's motives were unimpeachable. I do not censure him, knowing that in my own student days I might as easily have made similar errors. The whole sorry tale, however, underlines my previous point: unless and until the anthropologist can find some way of rendering himself invisible, even a chance and solitary contact with unknown peoples (if such still exist) will invariably be as devastating in its result as a full-scale, genocidal invasion . . .

From the Autumn Lecture Programme for the Friends of Buriton University:

Professor Thea Crawford, MA, PhD, FSA.
Treasure hunting: an archaeological will-o'-the-wisp.

From Radio 4, The World At One, Christmas Eve

Reports are just coming in of a spectacular archaeological find in an uninhabited jungle area of North Western Brazil. A team sponsored by the Australian-based Grail Foundation claims to have found the long-lost city of El Dorado . . .

RO127874242 humca M
Mann, Jessica
Faith, hope, and homicide
RO127874242 humca M
Houston Public Library
Humanities
MAY 91